Claiming One

E.J. Runyon

First Published by Inspired Quill: January 2012
This Edition: February 2019

Amended Edition

Editors: Peter Stewart, Sara-Jayne Slack, Laura Cayuela Ferrero
Cover Art: Zoe Amory
Cover Design: Venetia Jackson
Typeset in Adobe Garamond Pro

Paperback ISBN: 978-1-908600-06-6
eBook ISBN: 978-1-908600-07-3
Print Edition

Printed in the United Kingdom
1 2 3 4 5 6 7 8 9 10

Inspired Quill Publishing, UK
Business Reg. No. 7592847
www.inspired-quill.com

Praise for Claiming One

Runyon tells her stories with an unashamed truthfulness. The work is edgy, but never gratuitously so, never for the sake of edginess. At the same time, there exists a compelling emotional accessibility. If you are willing to risk reading, it will challenge you, capture your attention, and dare you to continue till the very last.

– Catherine Ryan Hyde,
author of *Pay it Forward* and *Jumpstart the World*

With this first collection, Runyon is following in the tradition of the great regional American writers. Flannery O'Connor, John Fante, Bret Harte, and Sinclair Lewis. The triumph of their stories was due in part to the writers' craftsmanship and vision, but also to the honesty of the narrative which grounded the fictive worlds deeply in reality.

– Adam Burgess,
owner of *Roof Beam Reader*

For NCG

Who let me in, from the first.

WARNING: REAL LIFE AHEAD

Step into these 17 worlds. Into lives as they are lived. These are the people you recognize on buses or in cafes. The people you might disregard because of how they live, or who they love.

At one time or another, a story can be told about any of us. Recognition may be discomforting, but don't fear it.

Take a chance.

Don't look away.

TABLE OF CONTENTS

The Giant Rubber Gorilla

My VOICES'RE ALL on the inside, afraid to come out. They know all the words. It's the pronouncing that stops them. They don't scare anyone (like some of the women on my floor at the Hotel scare me). But when you only see words inside your head, how can you be sure you're saying them right? Saying things wrong is worse than not saying them at all. My aunt Lillian can stare holes through a person if they don't say things in just the right way.

Gina and Aunt Lillian think I'm just their crazy second cousin, waiting in Gina's backseat for my weekend ride, up and down dreary streets going nowhere, like walking some cooped-up pet. Too many voices in my head to be kept at home and too young for the old folks' residence.

When my daddy left and my mamma started in with her razor blades, I moved into Aunt Lillian's house to stay. I slept in a tiny bed in Cousin Gina's room when we were both small.

Aunt Lillian never should've shown me all Gina's fifth grade spelling papers and grammar homework. When I proved to be good at it, she threatened, "I'll show you, missy, too smart for your own good." Now I believe I got so far ahead of myself, there's this blank space where I never got around to being me. I think they hate me for it now.

Gina stops for gas at the corner. She pumps, then sticks her head in the driver's side. "Mother, you want a Coke?"

Lillian takes off her lady's pastel hat, fussing with her seatbelt like Gina hasn't said a word. She tries to reach for the radio knob, but her wrinkled arm won't go that far, strapped in like she is.

"Mother, a Coke?"

Lillian breathes out so hard the hanging rainbow car deodorizer twirls in the sunshine.

"Mother, yes or no?"

Lillian grunts, straining towards the knob. "Get me one of them big ol' mushies. Make it red."

"Slushy. They're called slushies."

"Like I got to explain myself to you, Regina Raeanne. You know what I mean. Who do you think you are, your father?"

Gina's head backs up at this. "Okay, a red one." Then, about to turn, she leans again. "Anything to eat?"

"We can wait for a Jack in the Box."

Gina pulls her head all the way out, not catching my eye. She walks away. Then Lillian twists in her seat, shouts out the window, "Regina! Nothing for this one. I don't want to stop ten times for bathroom breaks."

Through the rear-view mirror I can see Gina doesn't turn around. She nods, her hand out behind her, waving Lillian's shout away. *I know, I know.*

That leaves me and Lillian in the car. If my good voice was working, I'd say something to her and she'd laugh. I'd say something right; maybe she'd turn around and smile at me. But Mrs. Farr at the Board and Care Hotel took my good voice. She's using it to make obscene phone calls to the government, so it's all slimy now.

I want to tell Lillian that Mrs. Farr's embezzling all my SSI money, so there's hardly any left for English muffins. Not even the plain type. If I had my good voice, I'd be sitting in the front seat with Lillian right now, driving around, pointing out places I used to work at, last time I was well.

Gina's shadow hits me before the sound of her shoes do. But I don't flinch; she'd never hurt me. She slips me a soda; quiet, low, out of Lillian's line of view. It's nice and cool. I like the feel of the can on my fingertips.

We pull out of the station and head to the freeway. Store signs, other cars, people on the street, all moving faster than I can settle anything in my mind. When we get to a yellow light the car slows. I can align my eyes for a second. A white and red sign on the lawn of a dirty stucco house reads: *Deepwater Bail Bonds – Open 25 hours.* Then the car starts moving again. Aunt Lillian asks, "So, what's on the agenda, today?"

"You tell me, dear."

"You're driving, missy."

"Well it is my car, Mother."

"Like I don't know it's yours?" Lillian says. "Honey, you never let me forget it."

Gina makes a strangled noise in her throat. Her hand reaches behind her head, smoothes down the short curls at her nape. Then her fingers tuck the flag of the clothes-tag flat into her T-shirt. Gina used to ask me to do that, when she was fifteen and I was ten. She'd let me into the backseat for rides without Aunt Lillian. Gina's neck was always so smooth. I'd volunteer even when there was nothing to fix.

Aunt Lillian snorts and clamps her teeth down on the straw sticking out of her slushy. I hold the coldness of the soda to my wrist; numb myself to ice. One of my voices whispers: *She's right, you know.*

Gina reaches for a button on the radio. "You want that personal achievement station? It's on AM."

"Find me some music with no words."

"Jazz?" No answer from Lillian. "Mother, Classical?"

"Oh, whatever." Then Lillian pushes out more air, complaining, "what's the rush, lead-foot? It's Sunday, slow down."

At the next stop sign we pass a junkyard. Rusted body parts lean up against the chain links like they're begging for release. Gina says, "Mother, let's not take the freeway, let's drive down Amstead all the way to the beach."

"OK, let's stop at—Lord. What is that, a boy or girl?" Lillian's pointing to a figure we've just passed, in white make-up, black t-shirt and jeans.

Gina chuckles as she glances at the kid. "That's a who-cares-anyway."

"You can say that again. And I thought you were bad

with your teenage *shinola*. Lord." Lillian's eyes follow the kid, until she catches me in her line of vision. Deep lines like old wounds run across her forehead, and down from the corners of her mouth. Then she frowns, faces front again. "Why don't they try church instead of street corners? What that kid's mother must be going through."

Gina watches the kid out of her rear-view mirror, "Looks like it's a girl—she's flirting with a skinny boy—perfect match."

"Just 'cause it's flirting with a boy doesn't mean squat these days, you should know that." Gina makes that throat sound again, keeps her hands on the wheel. The car speeds up until Lillian grabs hold of the rubber strap above her window, saying, "Anyway…"

In the silence Lillian touches the top of her bun. She lowers her chin to her chest and stares, near-sighted, at the flower-print on her left shoulder. Picks something off with her fingertips like she's weeding some delicate fabric garden.

"How about we go to Big Biffy's for lunch? They got a new one with a yarn store two doors down. I need some 'F' hooks for the afghan we're crocheting at church."

Gina slows down a bit, tilts her head. "Sounds like a plan, but not a sound plan." She nods to me. "She won't stay in the car after lunch."

Yes I will.

Lillian sighs. "Then let's go to the yarn shop first. We'll come get her from the car after, for lunch."

"Yeah?"

They think awhile. Lillian says, "Nah, let's just skip the yarn shop; I'll get the hooks later. Lacy said she'll be by during the week."

"How's she doing? Gene still holding on?"

"Just barely, poor man—at least your father had the decency of *wham*, dying all at once."

In their silence, my head fills with whispers I can hardly feel. Gene, Lacy's husband, is dying, the same way Gina's dad did. I try not to listen, but faintly, like the scars from all my operations that Mrs. Farr insists I haven't had, I hear singing in my head: *foul decay, run away, lost kiss, last dismiss, here today, slow decay, late for lent, desiccant.*

I *would* have stayed in the car while they went for yarn.

There's a giant rubber gorilla tied to the roof of a building. Its arms are outstretched; they look pretty strong. I want to climb the roof, have the gorilla be mine, to protect me, to listen to my voices. So I can go out on my own, without Lillian. But it's staring out into the distance; we don't make eye-contact.

Gina doesn't take the next turn like she needs to, to get to Big Biffy's. "I don't know. I'm not hungry yet," she says. "Let's just drive around awhile, okay?"

"Well then, turn off that air conditioning." Lillian rolls her window down, sticks her elbow into the breeze. "What a glorious Sunday," she says to the trees.

Lillian is pointing out all the jacaranda trees lined along the streets.

"They're heaven to look at June through September." She breathes in big, her face to the lavender umbrella over us. "You ever see such beautiful trees?" She sighs again.

"Little white bunnies and chicks all sitting in the carpet of purple underneath," she turns her face to Gina. "'course, I heard the roots get all into your plumbing. Right into everything. Screws it all up. Wouldn't want one in my yard."

Gina mumbles about roots doing just that. She doesn't look over, like she's not even said anything at all. They both ignore the mumble, like they do me.

We slow to a stop at a light. While we wait for the car in front of us to take its turn, Lillian fumbles her slushy cup and it falls out the window, bouncing against the tail-end of a white hatchback that's come up fast on our right. The white car screeches around the corner. I catch a glimpse as it goes, a big splash of red slushy on the bumper.

"Mother!"

"It was an accident," Lillian says, turning with surprise to Gina. "Honest. Oh, my Lord." Then they both start giggling, high, tinkly—like trembling nerves when you've sprinkled glitter on them so they'll show to the light.

Our light's changed. Gina's flying on through the intersection, watching through her mirrors for the bloodied car to come get us.

My can of soda rolls right off of my lap when she slams on the breaks at the next stop. It rolls out of sight under Gina's seat and stays there. The sound and lightness of their laughter hang in the backseat over my head.

Gina teases, "Wait till I tell Lacy and all the quilt ladies what a vandal you are. They won't let you near their babies at Bible preschool once this gets out."

"Gina," Lillian laughs, "I swear, I didn't even see him

coming." Holds her hand to her chest, "Oh, Lord!" She reaches up with a single finger to wipe at the corner of her eye. Patting at the air an inch above Gina's arm, Lillian shifts her bottom in the car seat, leans into the space between. Without taking her eyes off the road or turning to Gina, she lowers her voice. She's grinning at Gina, and Gina, she's smiling. Nodding, too.

I don't get it. Never have. If I laughed at Lillian, she'd've slapped me so hard, a hiss in her voice—*you don't exist*, and I'd have to make myself disappear to hide myself. But here they are, off giggling. I listen. Nod. Though I'll never know what it feels like to really know why.

"Jack in the Box," Lillian says.

Gina shakes her head, "Carl Jr. is right up on Powter. They've got a salad bar."

"I don't like their drive-thru; they tacked it onto the building all wrong. Bass-ackwards, I have to do the ordering."

"Okay, then I'll park and go in and order. I can make me a salad."

"Well," Lillian says, "get me a Chicken Club Combo. I'll share mine with her. No ice in the Dr. Pepper."

We pull into the parking lot; Gina stops the car right up against the wall-wide windows. They reflect the sun so our car looks like it's inside, eating fries, slurping malts with the families in the booths. Gina gets out. Aunt Lillian tells her, "Gimme your keys, I want to hear the radio."

Lillian's watching Gina's every move. Her head works left and right, like Gina's remote controlled. Lillian only glances away when she sees Gina walk toward the salad bar with her plate.

Gina circles the salad bar, head down. Choices.

A redhead's at the opposite end of the bar, she and Gina both move toward the middle. When the woman reaches for the same tongs Gina's going for, their hands must have touched because they both pull back, look up at each other.

Gina's putting her arms out, hugging like they're old friends, two plates held out behind two backs. Now Lillian is muttering, "Damn. Oh, Hell. What does she want?" Gina glances to the car then sets her back to us, talks to the short redhead longer. Lillian's muttering curses until a boy hands Gina her bag of food in exchange for her number. Gina leans into the woman and kisses her cheek before she turns to come back.

Now Gina's eyes are on her feet as she walks. Her salad plate's half empty; she's forgotten a lid. Lillian's food bag swings from her fingers under the plate. Gina touches the back of her neck with her free hand.

"In public? On a Sunday? You talked to that—in public? What is in your head, girl?"

"Mother, Jo is—"

"Nope." Lillian cuts her off, "don't even speak." She yanks the food in through the window, hisses, "Gimme my change."

"Mother—" Gina stands, motionless. Then she breathes out like it hurts, "It's in the bag." She walks around; past the headlights, like crossing a stage. Me and Lillian watching some show.

I see Gina's ears grow redder as she waits in her seat, not turning the key. No voice on the radio. She tips the salad out her window, lets it slide off the plate, lets the plate slip from her hand too.

Gina starts the car up, looks over her shoulder to pull out of the parking space. Our eyes meet. She glances beyond me, eyes guilty from more than just this Jo. I keep watch on our window; that redhead's taken a seat, but the trick of the window puts her in the back of our car, right next to me. As Gina pulls out the woman drops away, then she's gone. A whole new voice calls out to me, familiar; *am I to blame?*

Gina's ears are still red, even after Lillian's stopped hissing every few seconds. Once in a while Gina stomps her brakes hard; scolds drivers to 'pick a lane, buddy, pick a lane'. Swerves more to pass cars on their right, won't wait for traffic to speed. Finally she turns onto a quieter street. I'm hungry. Lillian still has hold of the food.

We drive aimlessly. Gina and Aunt Lillian are silent. Their giggling left blocks behind.

"Shit! Squirrel!" Gina shouts. She tries to slam on the brakes but something's wrong; they're not taking, and she ends up pulling the wheel sharp to the right, slamming the car into a rank of garbage cans in the gutter.

Lillian yells, "What the—" holds her hands out to stop from banging into the dashboard. I stretch my legs out to the seatback but slip; fall over, the seatbelt digging into my side.

Lillian is yelling again. Gina is crying. She twists, bends, reaches under the steering column; little tinny sobbing noises.

"You okay, baby?" Lillian asks.

Gina straightens out, comes up with my soda can in her fist. Dented but still unopened. "Under the brake." Tears still streaming down. She pounds on the steering wheel. "God damned can. Goddammit. God damned lousy squirrel. Fucking-goddamned-mother-squirrel."

She goes on and on like that. Lillian reaches over, gives her a good slap. Hard. My voices all start up at once, reporting the news: *Wow. She finally touched Gina.*

"Get a hold of yourself. It was only a squirrel. That's all."

Gina brings her hand to her cheek. The smell of Chicken Club Combo is in the air. Green from the trees shines in from the windshield. Something bad is happening now, something I can remember but don't want to. Gina breathes in, speaks in a low, calm voice, "Mother, that was my Jo."

"No." Lillian's head shakes.

"Yes. That was who—"

"Gina, I'm warning—"

"Mother—"

"No." Lillian shakes harder now, all of her.

Be quiet, I think, *don't say it, Gina. I'll get in trouble again. She just caught us that once, but look what she did to me for it. Just don't say anything. Please, Gina, please.*

"Yes. That's the Jo I was living with at school." She grips the steering wheel, looks through the windshield. "Not Joseph, Josie."

"You want me out of this car this minute? Do you? This won't happen, damn you. Not again."

Gina turns, looks at Lillian through the green. "I don't—I just don't care anymore. Maybe you can ruin…" she tilts her head to me, "but not me. No more."

Lillian catches a breath, holds it tight, but has to finally let it go. Turns her face to the curb. Gina starts the car, drives.

We pass the gorilla again. This time I wave.

At the Board and Care Hotel, Mrs. Farr stands at Gina's door, grabs hold of me as Gina pulls her seat forward; leans, so I can get out the backseat. Gina looks me right in the eye, says low, "Maybe we'll go for a ride by ourselves. Wednesday."

I turn as Mrs. Farr asks, "Ain't you gonna say bye?"

One of my voices tries. "Uh-huh," it mumbles to the car roof. "Bye. I had a nice gorilla." Mrs. Farr makes a *phuff* noise in my ear. And I turn then, back again. It's hard. But I bend, lean my smile in, at Gina. I touch her shoulder, gentle.

And right out loud, it's me.

I say, "Wednesday."

Fairest Of Them All

I T TOOK HOURS to find the exact shade of blue shirt he used to wear back when he was the assistant manager for the Globe Tire shop in Torrance. But Buddy Wyatt figured his best girl was on her way. So he'd taken the time after work on Wednesday, searching through shops in the mall. He'd given up on finding a polo and settled for the t-shirt.

Even after Buddy cut away the tag at the neckline and stood pushing the mirror on his bedroom door forward and back to catch the most of the ceiling light, it still didn't fit like he expected. He wasn't the trim twenty-eight year old he'd been the last time Cinda had seen him, eight years ago.

At the Safeway, after the mall, he'd been forced to put back the full-sized bottle of conditioner after he'd already handed over the six-pack, and the total was still a dollar and thirty-seven cents over the seventeen dollars in his pocket. But he still wouldn't exchange the small bottle of Old Spice aftershave. He was sure Cinda would want him smelling just like he used to. After the conditioner was subtracted, the new total fit his funds, and his change came to sixty cents. He scooped out the two quarters and the dime from the automatic change maker and handed them back to the cashier, asking for nickels instead.

"I've got big plans for the three-day weekend," he told the bank-teller when he cashed in three of his fifty-dollar bonds. "I'm taking a trip down to the Renaissance Faire, out in San Bernardino." The teller had glanced at Buddy but kept her eyes level with his chin as she counted out his bills, so he didn't add that it would be his first time there, or that the weather guy on TV warned of showers. Buddy expected the trip down the 58 from Bakersfield to be a nice, sunny ride. The high desert in all directions, monument-sized rocks to point at, and if he got lucky, maybe tall fleecy cumulus clouds; Cinda had always gotten a kick out of those. *Plenty of time for conversation, too*, he thought, grinning as he remembered old times.

Friday evening Buddy spent time vacuuming out his '74 Maverick. Then he took an extra hour on his knees in the driveway, polishing the rims, and then burnishing the dash, door panels, and the bench-seats, front and back.

The sun was long gone by the time he'd gotten home from work. So Buddy had started on the car without eating dinner. Standing and stretching when his back stiffened and threatened to lock up, then kneeling again till he made the blue Naugahyde gleam. He whistled through his teeth when he stood back for the last time, pushing his sore knuckles up into the spot of pain in the small of his back, finally satisfied.

In the morning Buddy showered with a new bar of deodorant soap, and washed his hair twice through before using a palmful of pearl green conditioner squeezed from the three-inch high sample bottle. After his shower, he waited. His eyes on the sunny street outside his living room window. Buddy stood a few steps back, in the room's shadows so he wouldn't seem too eager. *Long time,* he thought as he smoothed the flats of his hands on his new Levi's. He plucked at the neck of his t-shirt, suddenly wishing he'd bought something nicer for the occasion.

He sat, absently stacking and un-stacking the cork and acrylic coasters on the coffee table, when he heard a car in his drive. The practiced repartee he'd been running around in his mind froze. He paused in the center of the room, waiting to answer the sound of a knock on the door.

Except no-one knocked. Buddy tiptoed into his bedroom. Standing on his mattress, but gaining only inches from the floor. He stretched on his toes and peeked sideways through the high blinds at the windshield of an unfamiliar car in the drive. Buddy's ex-wife, Sue, sat behind the wheel. A slim-faced young girl with jet-black bangs showing under a gray ball cap slumped low next to her in the front seat. *Where's Cinda,* he wondered, *asleep in the back seat?*

The dark-haired passenger was shouting something at Sue. Then both of them sat scowling at the windshield. After a wait, Sue reached into the back seat and pulled forward a duffel bag and started the car, gunning the engine. Her passenger stepped out, slamming the door, swinging the bag at Sue and the car as it slipped out of Buddy's driveway.

Cinda, black-haired, (sixteen years old now, she reminded him) *this* Cinda sat at the edge of Buddy's Lay-Z-Boy chair, flipped the handle to let the seatback down. She tossed bored answers over her shoulder to Buddy's stunned questions as they came from the kitchen where he'd fled. He wasn't sure, because it had been so long, but from her tone, Buddy feared he was being made fun of.

When did she change to this—person?

"Friends?" she asked, "Oh, yeah, me an' Hildy and Buffy go out all the time."

He watched from over the kitchen counter as she unfurled herself, deep into the flattened recliner. "Miniature *golf*, you know? It's a *gas*."

Buddy returned to the living room, sneaking quick peeks. Her black bangs covered her plucked eyebrows; her chin on her slight chest. The recliner had nearly swallowed her narrow torso. Cinda's knees were the only part of her body, aside from her neck, that was bent.

He set a can of soda on a coaster and backed away until the bottom of his calves bumped his plaid sofa, stopping his retreat. The cap on her unnerving black dyed hair read 'Cin' in red embroidered script.

"There's the soda," he told her knees; the highest point on the recliner.

"No beers?" Cinda asked, eyeing the can over her knees. "Susan says, like, all you live on up here is beer. Jeez. At least, I thought—y'know—there'd be beers." Not quite under *her* breath, speaking into her horizontal chest, she added '*Jeez*'.

She ignored the soda and absently drew her left knee, the one nearest Buddy, up to her chin. Cinda scratched at her ankle with short-bitten nails painted a glossy shade of bruise purple. A small, neat tattoo peeked out from under her busy fingertips: a tiny green frog.

Buddy twitched, bumping his shin on the coffee table, and coughed, "Uh. Let's get on the road. Okay? We, uh, we got a ways to go."

Cinda shrugged, rose in slow motion, ignored the fizzing can of soda, and followed. Her duffel lazily banging against the new red splotch on her pale ankle.

Buddy held off stopping for food until they reached Tiffany's Coffee Shop, off the freeway, just past the Wrightwood exit. In his mind he'd envisioned how it used to be on their twice-monthly visits, that first year after he'd left. Cinda in her weekend dresses, holding tight to a miniature faux-leather pocket book on her lap; the way she'd sit tight in the front seat till he'd come around to her side and grandly open the car door for her. Her little legs stuck straight out on the seat. Her socks always matched her dresses.

Buddy figured maybe if she knew their destination was Tiffany's a smile might break. "Guess where we're stopping for lunch, Cinderella?"

At the pet name Cinda pushed herself closer to the passenger's door, snorting. She nodded to the back seat. "You got any beers in that cooler?"

Buddy thought about the check-out shuffle at the market, "No—but I smell good."

Cinda turned to look at him in confusion. A laser stare zeroed in, piercing between his brows, then passed right through him. Her feet wiggled, annoyed, against the dash. She turned her eyes back to the road, only moving to heave out breaths and punch radio buttons with the toe of her shoe.

Buddy finally gave up, and it was then that Cinda began to talk about the Faire.

"I can dress up, maybe. It's not much, but I got my shawl — in my bag? It's a skirt actually, a wrap-around skirt? Yeah, I made it in Home Ec." She bobbed her head to a song and added, "with a fringe." In a strange hopping move she knelt and reached behind the seat where she'd hurled her duffel, feeling around the cooler, picnic blankets, and all the other gear Buddy had packed the night before for their trip.

Buddy's peripheral vision was abruptly full of Cinda's rounded behind and her slim-jeaned thigh. A ragged tear, the size of a knothole, was distinct at the jean's seam, eye level, revealing freckled skin and a slip of black underwear. For a second the car pulled, jerking on the road. Buddy ran over a few lane reflectors before he regained control.

Cinda's body rocked slightly as she hung over the seatback, still digging for her duffel. She continued her muffled description of the shawl/skirt. "I got a B-plus on it. 'Cept it really doesn't go with my top," her voice clearer as she plopped back into sitting position, this time closer to Buddy than to the door, "'cause you don't wear white with cream." Two vertical lines deepened between her brows as she shook a crumpled piece of fringed white cotton out on her lap, pressing it out with the heel of her hand. "I'll have to leave my hoodie in the car, I—" She stopped and smiled. "Hey—you *do* smell good." Cinda brushed at her bangs, her eyes eight years old again, turning to him for a reaction. Buddy nodded and gave the shawl a nervous thumbs up. He cleared his throat, twice.

In the coffee shop parking lot, Cinda was out of the Maverick before Buddy had set the emergency break.

"I'll have the bacon-burger," Buddy told the waitress, "and—you want one of your girl-cheese sandwiches, Cinda?"

Cinda frowned, her face growing pink right up under her black bangs. "My what?"

The waitress shifted, exhaled. Buddy felt the few points he'd gathered wing away from him. He back-pedaled, "Uh, what'll it be?" He focused on the menu, "anything 'cept a beer." He grinned to the waitress, but by then she'd stepped away to the next table. Buddy looked back to Cinda. He leaned in to ask, "You don't remember how you used to go over the menu, looking for words you knew?" He tapped his keys with his fingertips. "You thought it was called a *girl-cheese* sandwich. That was your favorite order, with orange juice?"

"Buddy—" Cinda snatched her hands from the table, holding them down in her lap. She rounded her shoulders and stared out at the asphalt of the parking lot. "Jeez, I was just a stupid kid then."

"You were never stupid, Cinda." Past her shoulder Buddy noticed a tall glass display case near the door. It was full of fancy dolls, dressed in Indian squaw, Spanish dancer and Dutch-girl costumes. One doll was a mouse in a wedding dress. "I always thought you were pretty sharp."

"Well, you were my *dad*."

Buddy thought about Cinda's frog tattoo and wondered: *What am I now?*

On their way out of the coffee shop, Buddy paused and fished into his pocket. He handed Cinda two nickels.

"What's this?"

Buddy's gesture turned feeble as he pointed to the gumball dispensers, "For the machines."

"Oh, Buddy—" She pushed at the glass door and stepped out into the sunshine, shaking her head as she walked to the Maverick. Buddy followed. Cinda leaned against her side of the car, waiting for Buddy to unlock it. She flipped a nickel up into the air, smiling down at the asphalt and then flipped it again. As Buddy opened her door, Cinda slid into the seat, whispering, *"Girl-cheese* sandwiches. Jeez."

Cinda leaned her head out the window, the wind pushing her hair from her face. She stretched, her bare feet propped up on Buddy's dash. Her toenails were painted the same battered shade as her fingers. Buddy asked, "So, is your mom still fighting with the housework?"

Cinda yelled into the wind, "She says she's got better things to do with her time than vacuum."

Buddy remembered several of Sue's *better things*; first it was a Craig, then a Joey, and then eight years ago the thing to end all things, Dave or Dan, some D-named thing. Buddy tried not to, but he had to ask. "What's his name?"

"Richard."

"He a nice guy?"

Cinda pushed more of herself out to the wind. Her back arched. "Mom's started to call him a real do-it-yourself kinda guy."

"Fixes things?"

Cinda grinned to the sky. "She told him about the screen door. 'Cause y'know, the cat hangs on it all the time? So the screen's ripped? So, Susan wanted him to replace the whole door." She giggled, her toes curling.

Buddy pictured a weak-shouldered guy with Band-Aids on his thumbs, not Sue's type really. "And?"

"Richard told her 'Lady, the only way to get that door replaced is to do it yourself.'" Cinda let loose a hoot and slapped her thigh, grinning up into the rushing wind.

Light splatters of rain began hitting the windshield as they drove into the Faire's parking area. They decided they'd come back for the cooler later. Cinda even let Buddy drape his arm around her shoulder as they ran to the shuttle bus that would take them to the gate. At the entrance's turnstiles, a Puritan stood waylaying faire-goers and pinning ribbons on those he caught: Fool, Peasant, Merchant, Lord. Cinda ducked away, but Buddy stepped right up.

The Puritan asked, "First time to the Faire, good Sir?"

Buddy nodded, his eyes bright with the game, and the dour Puritan tagged him a Fool for his willingness.

In spite of the slight drizzle, Buddy bought Cinda a lemon-ice, scooped back into its own hollowed, frozen half-rind. Further on, he selected a fairy wand, trimmed with pink ribbon roses. He pointed to nearly every stall they passed, but nothing pleased; her eyes only scanned the faces in the crowd, as if she was searching for anyone to be with, except him.

Then she pointed, taking hold of Buddy's hand for the first time. "Buddy, look. Incense." He grinned as she pulled him to the stall. "Jeez, I bet there's a hundred different kinds here. Look." She touched them, each stick and bundle, finally laying the tips of her fingers on the row of slim vials, as if for luck. "Oooh, lavender. Buddy, look."

Then Cinda noticed the merchant boy who waited in costume behind the counter. She averted her eyes, away from the boy and Buddy. She removed her cap and touched her hair. Buddy watched her smile back down at the rows of scents. The boy bowed, "Milady's wish?"

Buddy leaned his elbow on the counter watching the kid react to Cinda. *He must be sixteen. Seventeen tops*, Buddy thought. The boy stood a little taller. He aligned a vial, then another, as Cinda's fingers touched each label down the rows. With a quick tug he straightened the front of his merchant's costume, his eyes on every move she made. Buddy felt a pull in his heart and a tug at his gut. A strangely mixed sensation; both moving in opposite directions.

Cinda looked up through her eyelashes and asked the counter boy, "Are they *all* six dollars?"

"Six plus this." He tapped a hand-lettered card taped to the counter's planking at Buddy's elbow. It was nearly illegible. Old English script, hard to decipher for the flourishes:

The Queen's Tax: with all Scents

But Cinda leaned in to see the sign and laughed out. A loud, sour sound, "The queen's *box*? You got *that* in all of these? Forget it. No sale."

Mortification rose in the merchant boy's face, and Buddy could see the kid hadn't a clue where to let his eyes go. Cinda laughed again, then turned, swishing the ribboned wand, left, right; a cat's tail. She wandered away into the crowd. By the time Buddy had shrugged *sorry* and paid for a vial of lavender, Cinda was already lost from view.

Buddy spent several frantic moments scanning the crowd, then stopped. He had to laugh to himself. No wonder he couldn't find her, she wasn't blonde anymore. The sun made its way from behind a cloud as he retraced his steps, and remembering the merchant boy's face, he looked for a head of jet black now.

He found her, after a short search, hanging the receiver up in front of a bank of pay phones near the toilets. She jumped when she turned to find him waiting behind her. "Buddy!"

"Thought you lost me, huh?" he joked. He was about to reach into his pocket for the vial of lavender, but her frown stopped him. "What?"

"Nothing."

"C'mon, Cinda. What?"

She let out a puff of breath, "Why are we doing this, Buddy? What did Susan say to get you to do this?"

The question stopped Buddy cold. Sue had only said things he'd rather have forgotten, some true but certainly nothing he'd care to repeat to Cinda. Buddy asked, "You mean did she threaten me or something?"

"I mean did she tell you what happened? To me?"

Buddy shifted in front of Cinda, the hair rising on the back of his neck, he jiggled the nickels in his pocket. "What happened, Cin?"

"She didn't tell you I ran away? That they found me in the trailer park? In Oxnard? That they kept me there, those—guys?"

Buddy shook his head, no. What was going on? "It was bad? What happened?" Tears rose in Cinda's eyes, she moved to run. But he caught her arm. He tried to hug her thin frame. "You can tell me," he said, expecting the worst.

"No, I can't." She answered; giving him just that, as she ducked out of his reach again, disappearing back into the crowd.

It must have been an hour later when Buddy began to really worry that she might be lost for good this time. The rain had stopped and started in spurts, and his thoughts about Cinda's news jabbed and stung at him as he willed his mind to only work on scanning the crowd. What should he do about what she'd told him? What did she want, need? How was he going to tell Sue he'd lost Cinda?

A stall caught Buddy's eye. The vendor stood beside what looked like a scribe's table. There were inkpots, a small hand-press and feathery quill pens on the table. Calligraphied scrolls and t-shirts hung above the quill plumes. Two t-shirts hung side by side: *I'm with Milady*, and *I'm with Milord*, both with pointing hands, ruffles at the wrists, aimed at the other. The hand-lettered sign, pinned to a sample on the counter, read: *Master Scribe, Late of the Queen's Court. Offers four Words in his finest Hand.*

Buddy looked again through the crowds, left and right for a sign of Cinda. Nothing. He thought for a second, pointed to a pink tee with a low-scooped neck, wrote his four words on a slip of paper, then handed it across the counter.

The merchant read it and nodded, smiling. He bowed, hand on his heart, "Ah, good sir, ye possess the soul of a poet."

He began setting down iron-on script backwards onto the tee, humming *Greensleeves* as he worked. When the scribe was done, he reached under his counter and presented a length of ribbon. "To sweeten the sentiment, and perchance her gratitude as well?"

Buddy reached for the strip of pearlish-ivory ribbon, then stopped, "Have you got anything in red, maybe wine colored?"

"Ah, a rogue are ye then?"

Buddy took the finished shirt and folded the words in on themselves, then wrapped it around the vial of lavender. He tied the bundle with a floppy bow and tucked the small package into the crook of his arm; a surprise for when he found her.

He scanned up and down each path, but all he saw were children dressed in period costumes. Little ladies and lords, the boys wearing capes and swords, some grinning behind pointed beards. The girls in satins and ruffles. He searched and searched, but every booth he wandered into only contained echoes of Cinda at eight. Buddy didn't know what to do. He'd walked the entire circuit twice and was now back at the entrance. She seemed to be gone for good.

A voice from the front gate called out, through drops of light rain, "Make way for the street sweeper! Good maids and gentlemen, make way for the street sweeper!"

Buddy turned and stretched to see past the crowd. Bit by bit the other spectators parted, and Buddy saw a towheaded toddler. Two, three years old at most, dressed in a blue homespun smock, a rope tied under her arms, and a dusty rag in her little fist. Her father, at the other end of the rope, was the caller. "Make way," he shouted, "make way for the street sweeper!" The baby squatted, smiling, cheeks red and dimpled, and dusted at the ground. Happy in the drizzle, she duck stepped forward and dusted some more. The crowd clapped and tossed coins into the father's outstretched cap.

Then Buddy saw Cinda at the gate, leaning on a boy. No—a guy. He could see his brown sideburns from where he stood. And what Buddy prayed wasn't a leather jacket. He ran toward them, his chest tight, calling, "Cinda, Cinda wait."

Cinda pushed the guy, hurrying him through the gate. The crowd had fallen back in on itself, now that the tiny street sweeper had passed. Buddy had to push against them to reach Cinda. He finally caught up to the pair in the parking lot. Buddy bent, his hand on his knees, trying to breathe. "Cin, wait." He coughed.

It was the guy who stopped for Buddy, who told Cinda, "Wait here. I'm gonna get the bike." She stopped but turned her back to Buddy. Buddy stepped around to face her, but she only shifted again until she stood staring back at the entrance like it interested her.

"Cinda?" He wanted to touch her, to ask who this guy was. Where did she find him?

"Honey—" Buddy started.

"No, Buddy, don't bother."

"But what—who's—"

"Ray's a friend of Susan's, okay? I called him 'cause he lives out here. We're heading back to L.A. I'm going home."

"But you're with me." He asked more than stated.

"Buddy, you don't want to see me. If Susan didn't feel like Vegas for the weekend, and making me pay—for stuff, she wouldn't've even called you."

The guy, Ray, pulled his bike up as it began to rain harder. He stepped off and walked up to Buddy, "It's okay man, she'll get home all right. Cin, you want my jacket?" His voice was deep, but quiet, calm. Still the guy's leather frightened Buddy. Cinda shook her head, no.

"We going?" Ray asked.

Buddy saw then that he couldn't take him, even if he tried. He shook his head at Ray. *Can't you see she's mine?* Buddy's eyes begged. All he could think to say to Cinda was, "But I got you a surprise." He waggled the bundle under his arm. "The vendor said I had a way with words." *No that's stupid*, he thought. Buddy took a long breath. "I looked all over, Cinda. I waited a long time for today… for you…all over."

Cinda didn't reach for his surprise; she narrowed her eyes to the rain and leaned on Ray. "So you're waiting. I waited lots of times, Buddy. Even after Susan said why bother, I still waited." She stroked Ray's arm, in a way aimed at Buddy. "This won't kill you. It's not like you care."

Buddy hung his head, his tongue stilled. The rain was the loudest thing between them now. Finally he said, "I do care. Cinda, I've always cared."

But by now she'd taken a step away from him. Ray took her hand, and they headed for his motorcycle. She turned, raising her voice as she moved away from Buddy, a little skip in her backward step, "Buddy, if that's true you would've stayed. My friends care, you just dragged me here to make *you* happy."

Buddy's legs were moving then, and he caught up to the motorcycle in a few stiff steps. He grabbed for Cinda's thin arm as she began to straddle the bike.

"No. You're mine. My—"

Cinda jerked away from him and spat. "They tied me up there. There were *ants* crawling on my feet, Buddy! And I couldn't get away. Where were you then, *daddy*?"

In an instant Buddy dropped his hand. He lifted his face to her, but said nothing.

"What about your famous way with words, Buddy? Why don't you try that now? Huh?" She laughed, but not with a smile. "I'm nothing, Buddy. A nothing girl you don't know anymore."

"Honey—" Buddy stopped. He handed Cinda the pink package. Ray gunned his motor. The rain had begun to fall even harder, stinging.

Cinda wiped the drops from her face. "Oh, Buddy…" She pounded her fist on Ray's leathered back. As she did he popped the clutch, and the motorcycle bounced forward. Cinda grabbed for the sissy bar behind her, dropping Buddy's gift into the mud. Ray's bike leapt away. The rear wheel scattered mud on the red ribbon, until the small package was nearly lost under the muck.

Buddy waited there in the rain, silently willing Cinda back to him, but the bike only rode farther and farther away, and then so far that they were gone from his sight. He held the small of his back as he leaned down to retrieve the dirty bundle.

The inside's still good; that part's still clean, he thought to himself. He pulled the scarlet ribbon away and unfolded the pink shirt. He slipped the small vial of lavender into his pocket for safe-keeping. "She'll be back, sure she will."

Buddy stood in the rain, letting what had turned into a downpour wash the mud from the pale fabric. He held the gift out in front of himself at arm's length, and read his four words out loud.

Claiming One

S UNDAY, IN THE car after church, and she's still on about the comments that Ms. Avisian wrote about my Creative Writing Midterm grade. She keeps mumbling, *Nina's gotten an A in spite of herself,* like the words are dirty and she's cussing me out. My mom has a thing about our brains; my sister's and mine. We have distinctly different fathers, so Mom feels it must've all come from her. "Common denominator," she taps her own forehead, glaring at me via her rear-view, "the girl's got a hundred-thirty-eight point IQ," she tells the windshield. "That's no fifteen-year-old idiot, you know."

I'm nearly sixteen, actually. When I can't take it anymore I fall asleep and dream about a new mother. In my dream Ms. Avisian is my mother. I hand her my grade slip with all C's plus a D in conduct and still she kisses me full on the lips. Her face comes nearer and nearer till her dark hair is in my eyes. She says, "Nina, Nina," over and over again.

I wake up, sweating, and Nattie's leaning over the front seat, calling me. Shaking me. Saying my name. Mom's parked the car in the IHOP parking lot. I tell them, "Go eat." I pull my headphones on and stare out the opposite window into the Home Depot parking lot. "Leave me alone." I focus on stacks of paving stones. I want the dream back.

Mom stands near my window, gripping her purse strap like it's alive and it'll pounce. Her nostrils flare. I look away. She says to Natalie, "this must be a monthly thing." What an idiotic cop-out. They turn to walk to the restaurant. I sneak a peek. They walk apart from each other, like strangers.

I try to decipher the dream. I know all the things and people in your dreams are you, all of them. Whether you dream of pineapples or naked policemen, it's all part of you. What I can't figure is; did my dream mean I want to love my mother? Or do I want a mother I love?

Midweek, I say, "Hey, mom, listen," and read her a bit of news from the paper. About a new find in the solar system.

"Lovely," she nods, pouring another cup of coffee and adding milk. She runs her hand through her hair and sighs, "All new worlds and here we are stuck on this crappy one."

"Why do you think it's crappy?" I ask, setting the paper down. "What would make it better?" In a weird way I really wanted to know.

"I have no idea." Her lower lip pouts out, "No—I do." I don't see it coming at all. "The best of all possible worlds will be when you and Nat are out on your own and I won't have to worry about you. And obviously that'll be the day I'm dead."

Such crap, I think. "You'll be dead the day we're out on our own? Or on the day you stop worrying?" It's silly, teasing her like that, but it was just us two. I was in a good mood. I risked it, "Fear or wish? Which is it gon—"

But she doesn't laugh. She reaches across the table and yanks once on my hair, hard. "Think you're so prepared now? Think all it takes is brains and no common sense?" She sits back and sips her coffee. "Think you learned from all my mistakes and you're ready to take on the world now?"

Where did that come from? "Mom, I—"

She laughed. "Ay, m'hijita." she shakes her head. "You don't know shit about shit."

She reaches for the paper, "I'm gonna teach you to drive. No. No, first I'll get the car tuned up. Get it running right, that way if it goes wrong it'll be your job to figure out what it needs. Yeah, we'll start as soon as I get it tuned up. Okay, hon?"

We hear my mom coming down the hall and Ritchie turns a shade of pale I thought was only possible with special effects. I shove the still-wrapped condom and his belt into his hands then shove him into my closet and try to get to the door before she opens it and comes in. I open it just a crack, "Hi mom."

"Nina." She says, her hand propped on her own bedroom door. She wears her dark blue scrubs. I like that color on her. She pushes her hair from her forehead, tired.

"Forget Sunday. Saturday, I'm dropping off the car first thing, so be ready to drive by nine. I'll be back by then. Sharp." She thinks about it. "Have a good breakfast, you'll need it."

I know I should back down, with Ritchie in my closet with all the rest of the evidence in his hands, but I don't. Maybe I'm just not as smart as everyone thinks; "I'm not all that desperate to learn to drive, mom."

She comes towards me. "I'm desperate enough for the both of us. Saturday, dammit."

I laugh. "Yeah, you're that alright." She's gonna come in here any moment. That'd be curtains for Ritchie. "You know what your problem is?" My wrists are tight under my armpits.

"My problem! *You're* my problem!" Her voice echoes in the hall and we can hear Nattie's music go up higher.

"Not quite. Your problem is you're just—"

"*Cuidado, chica...*" she warns, stepping back, near enough to strike.

God, I'm stupid. Because now I can't stop. "You're just a... a... antiquated, sad woman and maybe that makes you desperate, mom." That stopped her.

"Antiquated? Antiquated? Why you little bitch. I'll show you antiquated." And for some reason she stomps off to the kitchen. I wonder if I'd crossed some mom line once and for all, and she'd come back with a knife, but she's gone and picked up the phone. I hear her from the bedroom; talking to one of the guys from the ER. I never knew her to be this loud and forceful when she was sober. It's so embarrassing. She comes back toward my bedroom, standing there in the hall, her foot holding my door open, the phone tight in her grip. Mom keeps talking loudly, but her eyes are on me. She laughs like I knew she never would for real, giving him a low chuckle. She hangs up. So false.

She throws the phone against the wall. It works; I flinch. Then she points at me through my door, "When I'm done with him I'm going straight to the mechanics. And you, you little shit, are going to learn to drive if it's the last fucking thing I ever do in this miserable life. Do you hear the words falling out of my mouth, Nina?" I shoot back a look she hates. Because she'd made me flinch. She turns and makes her way to the front door, slamming it behind her. The walls shake.

I put my finger to my lips and pull Ritchie out of my closet. He grins at me, not sure about this. I don't care; I shove him back onto the bed. Snap my fingers for the condom. He's breathing like me. "Your mom's gonna have my balls, Nina." I push his shirt up to his neck, 'cause that's the thing with boys; they want to do it even when they don't want to do it.

"We just have to be real quiet," I say, kissing the line of hair leading down his belly. "We can do that, right?" I pull my top off. He still doesn't know what to do with his tongue, though.

I thought it was mom. Shaking my bed, back from the mechanics and wanting to get going.

But the shaking was way too rough. And I open my eyes and see the trees out the bedroom window swaying like all mad crazy. Loud popping noises go off outside the window. My books jump from my shelves, then the whole bookcase goes over. I try getting out of bed, but the shaking keeps bouncing me back into the mattress. The bedside lamp dangles off the nightstand and leaps up and up like it's trying to get back in place. And then I think: *Shit. Richie.*

He's at the door with nothing on, holding just my pillow in front of him. Bouncing against the wall like an imitation of the lamp; "Ni-Ni-Nina! What the fuck?!?"

"Earthquake!" I yell, "Get under my bathroom doorway." I pull on a nightshirt; the shaking still going on. But I manage to finally scramble to Nattie's room and find her under her mattress like we'd drilled. I pull her out and drag her into my room with us.

"Where's mom!?" she yells, then, even louder, "Richie! You're naked!" She covers her eyes.

The shaking finally stops. We turn on the TV first thing. Well, Ritchie got his pants on and went on home first.

I say, "Mom's probably gone right to the ER. So we should just chill out." But Nattie isn't hearing anything I say. Aftershocks rumble through; big bad scary ones that send us running for the bathroom doorframes. We must count five of them, each so strong I wonder why the newscasters call them aftershocks. They won't stop using the word liquefaction. I hate that word after awhile. But Nattie won't turn off the TV. Was Mom at work? Overloaded and just too busy to call? Or was she still with him? That Jon guy, trying to teach me a lesson? Would she do that to Nattie too, just to spite me?

The sun's going down and we still haven't turned on any lights. The TV keeps using phrases like 'extensive property damage', '65 reported deaths' and 'loss of life could have been much greater had the earthquake struck on a busier work day'.

Nattie lies under her quilt with a teddy bear, the TV on and the radio going in the kitchen, the angle of the sun above her making those dust-mote ballets in its long amber beam. Her legs twitch. But that's all the movement she shows. The fading light from the window makes her seem like an art installation: *Girl Waiting, Saturday.*

Sunday, early, the phone finally rings. I try to get to it first, but Nattie beats me. She frowns while she listens. Then she sits on the sofa, the phone cradled in her neck, her hands in a prayer between her knees. I take the phone. "Hello?"

"Nina?" Someone asks. A man's voice, "Is this Nina?"

"Yes?"

"Uh, this is, your um… this is your… Phil." He says.

"Phil."

"Um. Yeah. Are you there with just your little sister? Are you okay?"

I couldn't feel the phone in my hand. Phil. I sit down next to Nattie. "Yeah, we're here." I wait.

"Well, hon, I, uh, we need you to give us directions to the address, to your house. We'll be right over."

She didn't have my name in her purse. In case of an emergency. She had Phil's number. I can't figure out why. We hadn't seen Phil in about eight years, but that was the number they called. When the morgue got around to phoning.

It was the car. My mom had gone first thing in the morning, right when they opened, to have the car in for the tune-up. It was up on the rack to lube it. The mechanic was in the back, picking out tires for a new set when the quake started. The man who owned the station told the paramedics that my mom was standing in the bay, where she shouldn't have been, flirting and laughing with the mechanic.

What the mechanic says is the car came bouncing right off the rack. The TV's still going. A news guy glances down at his papers, then up into the camera. "…A car up on lifts for mechanical work in an Eastside body shop dropped in the quake, claiming one."

Nattie's apologizing to someone in her dreams, "My mom's not home. Can't let you in." The room Phil's new wife, Elaine, has stuffed us in is filled with that pale blue tone you get at night. I'm wide awake, coming up with odd thoughts. I watch Nattie as she's working her way around in circles on her bed. Like the hands of a clock, there's a violent shift and she's at five o'clock. Her quilt slides off the bed and I slip out from under mine to pull it back over her. Nattie's not enunciating well but I can pick up some things in bits and pieces. Then she raises her voice. It sounds important, and I listen in case she's figured out the reason to the biggest question; why my mom?

"It's B – no. Wait!" she mutters, "The answer's twelve!" and she advances again around her bed. I'm not used to sharing a room with her, so I'm wide awake, listening to

Nattie's reasons.

The school shrink asks me to close my eyes and tell my mom what I didn't have the time to tell her. "Role playing," she explains.

I say, "If it's role playing why can't I be the mom part?"

And damn her, she tells me: "Sure, let's do it that way."

A period bell rings and I catch sight of Ritchie up ahead. I can pick out his ball cap from a distance. He fights through the crowd because I've stopped walking in his direction. I'm spending a moment role-playing that I'm sight impaired. My make-believe glasses, on the floor at my feet, ground to bits. I un-focus my eyes as he approaches. He cocks his head to the side, "Nina?"

"Richie?" I hold my hand out, moving antenna-like, side to side.

"What's this?" he asks. I want to reach for him and ask him for a hug. Weird.

I ask, "Wanna blow this pop-stand and walk to the bridge, get stoned?" He just reaches for my hand and leads me out of Building B, across the back of campus, like a devoted guide dog. We head for the freeway bridge behind the school.

"We're gonna fix you up in just a bit." Ritchie says, still holding my hand.

"Make me human again?"

On the apex of the overpass, he pricks at the silence with a question: "Aside from the obvious, what do you want most in the world?" I think a second; count the VW bugs that pass in my lane below me; there aren't enough.

He smiles. Warns that he's coming in for a hug, and I let him. No more words. I lean forward into it and exhale, even though the sound's so raggedy, so unused. Still, I let it out all the way. "Lemme clarify," he says, leaning back to look into my eyes. "What do you want that I can give you?"

"Nothing."

But then I clear my throat; breathe in through my nose, push the breaths out longer, real. In a voice the wind grabs at, I try again, "Can you teach me to drive?"

Ones At The Edge

GORDO DROVE RATHER sanely for a guy with a full-sized mattress set strapped onto his '71 Impala's roof. The rising sun struck his rear-view mirror at an annoying angle, but he was patient. It would move. With an open can of Coors sweating between his legs, four more cans cooling his ankles and his cousins' truant wife, Bernie, silent and still next to him, he steered westward.

Bernie hadn't exactly told her husband Carlos why she was going. She didn't need to. In the Counselor's office she'd only straightened her shoulders and, keeping her hands down in her lap, she'd said, "I can go for good, or if you'd rather, I can go for the summer. What's better for you?" It seemed easier on him that way.

She'd stared at Carlos' knees, because her eyes wouldn't move any higher, holding herself tight the way she did. If she unfocused her eyes the carpet did a neat switch of perception, the beige parts becoming borders for the green areas. She waited for his answer, concentrating on the squares of carpet. Never stronger than at that moment. Never surer she'd be dead by the time he pulled the truck into their driveway. But taking that deep breath and saying it out loud just the same.

The beads of her rosary slipping though Bernie's fingers in clicks were the only sound in the car. "Please, don't turn it on, okay?" she whispered when Gordo reached for the radio. She wanted what she wanted, so now Gordo found he felt antsier in the quiet than he'd expected to. But that was okay too.

She fingered the beads one by one. *The moment I moved out.* Repeated in her mind, with each click. *This day. I moved out.* The sunrise hadn't fully breached the horizon behind her yet. The quiet felt good. She loved the colors rising slowly around her.

The next bead brought a vision of herself just minutes ago, in her driveway, the still cool air against her neck. Taking one last look before getting into Gordo's car. Her forehead between her brows wrinkled into those two little up and down lines that Carlos liked about her. Her shoulders tensed as she ticked the items off on her thin fingers, squinting up into the dimness of the early morning hour. Carlos was not due home from his graveyard shift at the bottling plant for a while.

Bernie was still in a hurry to get going out of the

driveway.

Another bead clicked and she hears his voice: "I'll give you a check." Carlos had told her, "You give that to the guy and be sure you get a receipt. Don't let him say in month two that he needs any more. Got it?"

He'd sat on the edge of their bed watching her pull a small handful of underwear from the laundry basket, to add to her stack of summer clothes from the drawers of her bureau.

"I won't, Carlos."

"Better not."

The beads slipped though Bernie's fingers like holy water in a font. Gordo remained tranquil in the face of no music, one hand high on the wheel, glad there weren't tears to deal with, no tirades. Until Bernie let out that sound. A stifled whimper.

He felt its push, like a live thing. Getting under his sternum, the sensation ran down his arms to his fingertips, like his Impala shuddering and slipping out of gear that winter when his transmission was all jacked up.

Gordo glanced in every one of his rear-view mirrors before tucking his chin down for another sip of beer. He stared straight ahead. "You need somebody, you call me. Okay?"

After killing the first beer Gordo made a bold decision and a wide detour. He exited the freeway and headed up to an IHOP. North, up a ways on Figueroa, stopping because he said they needed gas. But it was really to get some food into her. She was way too thin. Had to turn sideways twice just to cast a shadow. Girls needed a bit of meat on them. *Pancakes*, Gordo thought. *Yeah, that's what she needs.*

Bernie sat, hunched. Her short stack missing only a few token bites; for Gordo's benefit. Her wedding ring clinked once against her cup, louder in the empty seating section than it should have sounded. She looked at her hand like she'd just found it there on the table, a tip from the last customer. Nothing to do with her order at all. She slipped the ring off and into the pouch of her black hoodie. Then she started talking. Softly.

Bernie didn't consider herself a fugitive wife for two reasons: she touched the tip of her ring finger with her thumb, explaining to Gordo: "One. Carlos agreed to let me take the three months' rent plus deposit from his account."

She held onto that reason the tightest. Seeing Carlos' face as she looked off past Gordo's shoulder, *"You're gonna need it. Don't tell me no, Bernie."*

She didn't want to take anything from him that she'd have to come back and give him later. But Bernie kept that to herself.

The passing waitress broke her view of their bedroom and Bernie blinked, focusing on Gordo again. Her thumb to her middle finger now. Tapping this one, like it meant more.

"And two, you're a valid witness, Gordo. You saw what I've brought. Only the brass bed, my rocking chair, two boxes of books and my summer clothes."

Gordo nodded okay. "Sure." Wishing he had his beer under the table there. He added, "Hey, Bern, eat something, will ya? One more bite at least." Pushing her plate closer to her elbow. What else could he do? He could dawdle over a carafe of stale coffee, hoping she'd change her mind and ask to be taken back home, but in the end he saw; it was her story, she was sticking to it. They got back on the road.

Bernie had asked for the ride. And that's all Gordo was doing here. Giving the girl a ride.

"Hey, babe," Carlos had reached for her there in the bedroom, and pulled her to the bed, setting her between his knees and leaning his forehead on her middle, tender like he used to. "Just remember, you let me live like a bachelor, no telling how the house'll look come September." He smiled up at her and put his chin on her bellybutton, wiggling his eyebrows to make her laugh. Carlos; the good guy in this all of a sudden.

She tried not to pull away, tried to pay attention though her skin to all the things he was working to get across. But it was too late; she couldn't feel a thing.

Finally, there in the counselor's office, Carlos had answered: low, tired, no more patient breaths in and out. Giving in; "Three months, Bernie. No more. More- I-I couldn't take no more."

And the only thing keeping her from saying who'd had to take what so far was the ache in her wrist and the memory of coming to with her head up against the tile of the bathroom, where he'd slammed her that last time.

At the patio dinners the family had whispered about why they thought she was going, of what Carlos thought about it—just never talking in front of Bernie. Gordo ignored all the questions his side of the family burned to ask. Knowing they'd never ask Bernie directly. "You find out what the hell Bernadette's gonna do all by herself in the damn Hollywood," his aunt Arlene, Carlos' mother, pushed at the last get-together. "Is it a fella?" Gordo's dad whispered; his can of beer shaking in his palsied hand. "She likes you, Gordo, you find out, *mi hijo*."

"Nah, Linda. It can't be no man." Nadine was sure. The younger cousins, both girls, shook their heads over their plates of *pollo asado*. Babies on their laps, the two girls leaned in, eyes shining, like watching a *novela* on TV in the kitchen. Ignoring the shouts from their kids running through the sprinklers on the side of the lawn. "With Carlos? C'mon. This nice place? What more could she want?"

In the kitchen, Bernie's Aunt Maria had shaken her hand at her. "Here." Palm down and curled around something. "Quiet," she added, because the door was open to the backyard, the bougainvillea shining bright magenta in the sun. Green plastic chairs scattered under the jacaranda trees and the littlest kids running everywhere and screeching.

Bernie looked down at four folded one hundred dollar bills, unfurling in Maria's now up-turned hand like a green bud opening, then back up at Maria. Maria shoved them at her, "Go on." Then she picked up the biggest platter of tacos and bumped closed an open drawer with her hip as she walked out to the others, "Linda," she called, "get the sour cream, *Chula*, I got too much in my hands."

"Father Rudolph must be rolling over right now, mama," Nadine had joked. The women unconsciously hugged their purses closer to their sides as the three of them walked up the drive towards the bright red of the psychic's front door. Bernie never carried a purse; she had no car keys, and Carlos only gave her the money she needed for the exact errand she was allowed to go on.

"Father Rudolph's not the boss of me." Maria reached to the center of the red door and knocked.

Mrs. Ileana gave Bernie a look when she took hold of her hand, running her fingers over some of the lines on Bernie's open palm.

The three women sat and watched in the normal looking dining room (except for that money slot), and Bernie, nervous, made a closer survey of the woman now holding her hand.

She wore a woven jet black shawl; the coarse weave was shot through with iridescent threads—like she was wrapped in a starry night.

Bernie's hand trembled when the psychic shook her head, glancing quickly at Maria. Bernie was sure she knew all about the concussion and her wrist.

The psychic's tone was confident, "You're a person who'll gravitate toward the ones at the edge. The loners. The outcasts. But at your own detriment. Your own life will be in danger of going unrecognized." Nadine made a clicking noise with her tongue. Detriment, she'd said; was that

Carlos?

With all the lamps so bright in the psychic's living room, that wasn't the spooky part. Leaning in to see where her life was slipping away to, Bernie felt the pain rise up and leave her wrist, like naming the problem had relieved the ache. *That* was the spooky part.

Later, when they were out driving, Bernie tried to explain what it was like to Carlos, about how bright that red door was and how the spookiness felt, about the beautiful shawl. Not her nodding in agreement, not the pain miraculously lifting; "Gravitate," Carlos mimicked, and changed lanes too roughly, with quick jerks of the wheel.

Bernie, so lightweight, slid away from him on the truck's bench seat from his swerving. She was glad she hadn't thought of adding empathetic too, (the other thing the psychic had told her). Bernie's sore shoulder banged against the passenger's door before she could reach out to Carlos… to stop herself from falling away from him.

The apartment house she found was a three-story brick building that sat about six yards up from the edge of the Hollywood Freeway, just off the northbound Sunset exit. At the bottom end of a cul-de-sac, up against the constant rush of traffic sounds, where Antoinette Place and Lorenzo Way met. It was a fluke that she'd found it at all. Carlos had gone fishing up at the Santa Fe Dam with his Papi and his tío Raul and Bernie had the rare weekend to herself.

Nadine's call came practically before Carlos's truck had cleared their driveway. "Hey, *chica*, your mama says you're free this weekend, let's go get crazy while you got a chance."

Bernie liked Nadine, maybe more than any of the other cousins she'd married into. She always talked way tougher than she was. "Okay," Bernie agreed, "What's your preference?"

"For crazy there's only one place, baby." So they ended up taking Nadine's two boys and driving into Hollywood, first going up into Griffith Park with a picnic. Nadine's idea of crazy was anything that got her and the kids out of her own place. She liked the green. And she liked driving to find it. The apartment Luis had for them squatted, surrounded in browns, grays and tans, with mostly dirt out front and parking in the back. Right up next to the next apartment on the block was more dirt and more parking, and the next and the next.

"Man, this is the life, huh?" Nadine leaned back on her elbows on the quilt Bernie had thought to bring with them. Nadine stroked the black brush-cut hair of her youngest, Raymond. The seven-year-old laid in a C-shape next to his mom, his back to her thighs, shoes pulled off, toes in the grass, smiling, full of egg sandwiches, peaches and Fritos, almost asleep. Gilbert, Nadine's other one, was off sword fighting a tree with a branch he'd stripped from some bush along the path. It had been a walk to get to the picnic area from where they'd left the car.

"This is way better than the recreation center. This is nearly as good as your backyard."

Bernie shielded her eyes, watching Gilbert attack the

trees, resigned to the fact that this was as crazy as it got.

Later, Nadine headed down Western to Hollywood Boulevard, searching for even more variations of green. But she promised them Slurpies for good behavior on the drive back. So then Nadine and Bernie took their time strolling up and down some of the streets looking at the cool apartments in the little neighborhoods off of Wilton Place; bird of paradise flowers in nearly every yard. Lantana bushes spilling onto the sidewalks in knee-high humps of purples and yellows, occasionally a dividing hedge in a burnt orange color. Roses.

No Jacaranda trees, like in Bernie's backyard, but lots to see all the same. The architecture appealed to Bernie more than Nadine's need for green.

"It's like being back in the Forties," Bernie said.

"If you say so. You're the reader."

"I'm the reader too," Raymond piped in. And in a flash Bernie realized that she'd be going. Raymond, tugging at Bernie's hand as they walked asked, "What 'chu gonna do for the summer, Aunt Bernadette?"

She spun him in a circle in front of her, like a dance move, "*What're you* gonna do?" Nadine corrected.

"I'm gonna be in second when school goes again. I'm gonna be a reader too," Raymond tugged for another spin.

Bernie looked up into the trees, "I could use a break."

"Who can't?" Nadine said, "Gilbert Rios, you tear one more flower off one more bush and, *mi hijo*, you're gonna get it."

That's when they came to the apartment. Bernie just knew. There was a red and white FOR RENT sign in one of the lower windows and Bernie quickly spun Raymond around to face the other way. Away from the building. Suddenly superstitious. As if no one saw her interested, it might end up being hers. "Let's try this street."

She looked for a bus line as they walked back to Nadine's car and memorized its number. She came back that following day.

♦

As Gordo turned off Hollywood Boulevard onto her new street Bernie saw the loveseat and chair set in the corner storefront of a cheap furniture place, a big sign in faded red and blue on the window read: $259.95/SET

"Stop! That's it. I've been looking for that." Gordo swerved into the parking lot without a question and ten minutes later they'd arranged to pick up the two pieces after they'd gotten the mattress set unloaded. The stuff looked like play furniture to Gordo. But he wasn't the one who bought it.

Gordo didn't ask 'Why do you need a new loveseat? You've got a living room full of stuff at home.' And Bernie never made full eye contact in case he might.

♦

"The wrought iron on the back window's come loose," she'd told Carlos, setting a plate of fried potatoes and eggs down in front of him, using her good wrist with the heaped plate. It was a week before Gordo promised to drive her, "I was out in the yard. The stucco, it's crumbling around the bolts."

"Yeah."

Just *yeah*. Not a mean yeah, an empty one. No cross-examination on how the hell would she know from iron or stucco, crumbly or not? No grumbling or tossing his beer can extra hard into the sink to make her jump, no laughing at her words or complaining, "Shit, Bernie, what else?"

Just—yeah.

And now Gordo was saying she could call him if she needed to. Was the world gonna end next?

And now here she was. Moving in. A neighbor holding the building's glass doors wide for her and Gordo. The tall girl smiled. "Here you go," she said in a deep, smoky voice, then followed them in. She looked like she'd been out for an early morning stroll. Bernie's smile just grew and grew. Strolling.

◆

The neighbor asked, "What floor?" after Bernie introduced herself. And Bernie's smile just got wider and wider as it dawned on her. Here was this slim, nicely made-up girl/guy, in a pretty velour jogging suit. Wearing earrings even. Curly hair in a tidy cut: professional, looking down at Gordo and Bernie from about three inches above the top of Gordo's head. Her hands wide—no—wider than Carlos' or even his dad's. And a voice like a well, but with, what? A softness under the words? Sadness?

Bernie couldn't keep the bubbles of happy in her

contained. Just being so near. She stuffed her rosary in her jeans and squeezed into the narrow elevator, next to the sideways loveseat, the last of her boxes and the two full pillowcases. "Three."

She beamed, not caring if she was talking to a her or a him.

Bernie's forehead itched, but the little loveseat pinned her, so she shook her head, pony-like and puffed a breath up at her forehead. They caught each other's eye. And the guy/girl grinned at her. Bernie thought, *this is some new kind of freedom.* Here was someone from her own tribe, a tribe she'd only just realized existed. The strollers of the world. The readers.

Gordo sneezed. And for a second Bernie remembered who she was supposed to be.

◆

Standing alone now that Gordo had gone, she pulled her wedding ring from the hoodie's pouch. *Why didn't I bring a radio or tape player?* The silence around her felt like too much space in her head. She wasn't sure where to set her ring. It wasn't a safe silence like in Gordo's car. Maybe because here in this room everything was still, nothing rushing by on the periphery. The bumpy pale ceiling seemed too far away.

Bernie stepped into the little dressing room, slipped her ring into one of the big drawers, and heard the clunks it made as it rolled. She thought about setting up a pallet, from clothes and blankets, and sleeping in this small space, instead of in that big space out there. Too big for just her alone yet. That new big space left room for thoughts like: *Why are you doing this?*

The new carpet smell and the bare, cream-colored walls added to her sense of feeling detached, floating. And no matter how much Bernie's mind kept repeating, *What now Bernadette?* she couldn't be sure why she even kept asking.

While Gordo had been there helping, he'd gotten to work by pulling a screwdriver and a baggie full of bolts from his cargo pants and set up her bed frame and mattresses. He pushed it back against the wall, there in the corner away from the windows. "Nah, let's put it under the window." Bernie asked, "Can we?"

"There's no bars here, Bernadette," was all he said when she pointed to the other side of the wide room.

"Gordo, we're on the third floor." Bernie walked out pacing from wall to wall, front door to windows, head down, counting until she reached fifteen. *Just like Carlos*, she thought, *always for my own benefit. Yet never what I ask for.* Then she galloped across the room and, from the breakfast nook, paced to the closet alcove; twenty.

Three windows faced north. Her view, once she stopped with her pacing, stunned her into stillness. The hills rose and ribboned with pastel houses that peeked from the green in the distance. "Third floor's good," Gordo said, ignoring her stillness next to him.

She backed away from the window to get all three of the panes all in one view. "A panorama," Bernie whispered.

Gordo, standing silhouetted in the frame of the

window's light, hands on hips, just like Carlos always stood, ignored that too. "No freeway noise," he said. "You're gonna need food, Bernie." He bent for the screwdriver there on the beige carpet and straightened, stiff. First he reached into his pocket for the last can of Coors, then dug in another for his car keys. He popped the can and sipped, stepping back to the view and leaning to inspect the no-bars situation. "Lemme drive you now. You won't have to walk with bags," he told the windows.

"Sit." She patted the new loveseat. "Take a moment and drink your beer. Rest a bit, Gordo." Carlos hated any furniture with a pattern to the fabric, flowered prints especially, which was why she'd only taken her rocking chair, nothing else was worth sitting on. If Gordo tried sitting on this little thing his legs and knees would stick out. And Carlos was no taller than Gordo.

The new little loveseat's fabric, brushed cotton, looked like a metal-flake tan of a new truck, birds with wings wide flew and perched on Japanese-looking tree branches. The branches were loaded with mauve buds and flowers, like a water color scene, with shades of grays and blues.

Gordo looked at the loveseat, "I'm okay." He continued his patrolling of the room's perimeter.

"You need a chain for that door." He knocked his knuckle on the wall over her headboard. He flipped the switch in the tiny walk-in alcove, opening the built-in drawers and sticking his head in the bathroom. "Light's out in here. Get bulbs too. Or borrow one from that freak."

Meg. Bernie remembered her name. She ignored Gordo and his prowling, remained at the loveseat, stroking the satiny feel of the fabric, mentally planning how to rearrange the set around her rocking chair once he left.

She looked at the clock. He'd been home already now for five hours and eighteen minutes.

The little blue alarm clock Gordo had set up on an empty box next to the bed, for a nightstand, ticked and ticked.

The whole house would have been cleaned by noon, and on the days he worked his double shifts Bernie would only be there waiting for the moment to exchange the TV's noise for the sound of his truck pulling back out of the garage at 2 o'clock. Waiting so she could set herself in neutral until he came back. "Please God," she prayed out loud, in the middle of so little, "now that I've left him, let me be something grander than just that girl."

She yanked again and now the box spring slid off the frame and onto the carpet. She propped the top mattress on its side against the wall and bent to tackle the heavier piece next.

Mother's Tongue

I HAD TO tell Mari, "Don't ask me again," but she didn't listen. Kids. "You can see it. Why keep on?" I said. Just look at this one, so bossy for three. "You hold her," I said. "I'm tired." But she just wouldn't give up, dangling that howling baby in my face. A three-year-old and she was bugging me like my own conscious. Damn. "It's just a cough, Mari." I had to say that twice.

Her and her eyes. That look was as big a problem as the baby crying all the time. Never listening when I *told* her. "No, I don't wanna look at her. All new babies cough sometimes. Now go play with your brother."

How do you get this across? "You make her stop crying," I said finally. At least she wanted to touch her, stare into that face that shouldn't look like who it does.

How do you tell a toddler about men's pride and women who make mistakes?

"Make her stop crying!"

I know I yelled it. I know. I took a drag on my cig and stared at the wall, anywhere but toward that crib. "I swear I'll go crazy." Then the phone rang. "The nightshift? *Sí, bien*… Nah I'll find me a sitter… Well the youngest, she's six months… Oh yeah," I said over the cries, "—a big handful."

"Sure, sure," I told the sitter, small for fourteen, "back by morning. Well, the baby—she's loud. But Mari here's a great little helper."

I kissed the boy, my pride, and hurried on; places to be. Outside my door there's the damned *chismosas*, lined up along the hall just waiting to take a piece out of me. *Do your damnedest, you bitches*, I think. Maybe someday I'll say it out loud. At the bus I finally let my back un-stiffen. "Damn them all. *Pinche* projects."

"I promise, a last time."

Here's another babysitter giving me grief. But when a boss says you gotta stay what do you do? Pull the food from your kids mouths? "I promise, just once more with the late work." Maybe her sister can sit half the time. She's big for her age.

"Overtime, *ay!* … Just lemme call first." I dig into my jeans, angle my hip for change and the whistles start. I ignore them all. Troubles enough in my life. "Get this message to Rachel. The skinny one, *sí*." *Ay mi Dios*. "Well if she's not there, leave a note for me please."

"I promise, a last time..."

"I promise, just once more..."

"Well the youngest, she's six months," I tell the sister of that first one. I don't care what her age is. I got a bus to catch. "Sure, sure, back by morning." And out in the hall there they are again.

"You *pinche cabrona—*"

"What's it to you, some baby crying? That's what they do."

Home again and the first thing I get to say is, "I don't wanna hold her. You take her, I'm tired." Almost glad when the phone rings mid-day. "Overtime, *sí*... A phone call first, yes?"

So here I am begging. "I promise, just once more..."

Me begging. Why me all the time? "He left me, you see." And I grab up my purse, Mari doesn't even turn to say *bye-bye Mama* like she used to. I kiss the boy and the door snaps shut.

Out in the hall I really let loose. "Keep your nose to your own self, you barren old *bruja*." The howling for that and I just laugh.

I don't stop to hear it all. Same old song. Same ugly singer.

"Now who's that at the door?" I ask, still pissed that the sitter ran out on my kids. The boy out in the yard without his pants on, in January. At least the baby's not crying for once. And now this knocking at the door.

"Mr. Walden, from county," comes Mari's small voice, the perfect parrot with his card in her hand. Why did I never notice how small that voice was? And how come the baby's not howling?

"When there's three of them…" I try to explain. "Well, I tried…"

His clipboard gets more glances than me. But there's no way to explain how I didn't notice they had the baby already. That's where the blessed silence was from.

"Well, I ain't got a car." He sends the two kids into the next room and sets me on my own couch like it's his.

"Yeah, I understand fully… pneumonia. I got it."

Nobody told me. Nobody said.

"When there's three mouths to feed," I plead, I gotta go work. "Well, she just always cried."

But he isn't listening. He's all—"They'll all be placed. Today. Tomorrow at the latest." No room to beg here.

"But, I can't, I got work."

And I pledge to myself, if it's the last thing I do, that littlest one'll know what she did to her family; her brother and sister and me. I'm burning it into my head right now. This minute in time.

Someday she'll find me and ask, *"Mama, why did they take us?"* And I'll smile when I get to tell her.

"Well, you cried all the time."

Disappearance at High Noon

IT'S FAR AFTER midnight. Terry's shoved me into the back seat of the Yellow Cab that's come to take us to the emergency room. My wrists sting, like jellyfish burns. The rest of me feels numb. Even my brain seems lighter behind my forehead, and my ears are clogged, like I'm underwater.

She's standing on the sidewalk in the headlights, fighting with the driver while I sit, trying to press washcloths to my stomach with my opened wrists. I know I'm making a mess, but it looks a lot worse than it is. Vaguely their argument reaches me. I want to help, to explain, but I can't make any sounds of my own. Their voices float through the cool night:

"It's NOT a gunshot wound, it's just her wrists, dammit."

"Fuckin' crazy broads. Get her outta my cab." He's waving his hands, glaring at me through his windshield.

"It's what?" Terry begs, "Seventeen blocks maybe."

"—bleeding all over the place," he shouts, "shit—"

"—for Christ-sake, look." She pleads, holding out money. "You can have a happy Easter, I'll pay double."

The guy seems torn between the chance for a doubled fare and hating the thought of blood all over his cab. He pauses, taking his eyes off me. While Terry shakes money at him, coaxing him to drive us, I keep my head up, eyes on the transaction in the lights. His eyes are on the money; his shoulders sink as his hand reaches for the bills. With numb fingertips I reach into my jeans, sliding out the paper-wrapped packets. I toss their plastic container onto the floor of the cab, and slip the rest of the razor-blades into the leg of my boot.

You never know.

Terry's counting the blocks under her breath as our cab passes under sodium street lights, amber flashing dark and darker on our faces. I tried to get her not to come, but she slid in beside me, telling the cab driver; "You got your fare. Drive."

"You'll be in a world of hurt if you come in with me," I whisper.

Terry brings the tips of my fingers to her lips and says, "Your hands are so cold." She breathes warm breath on them.

Her eyes hold mine as tightly as her hands do, but I pull away, marking her with a smear of red at her chin. She looks down at the soaked washcloths. "Damn."

I say, "I just had to let out some of the pressure." I wince at my voice, louder than I expected, "Terry, you can't know me at the hospital. Just drop me off and go."

I feel the cabby's eyes on us in the rear-view mirror. As Terry's fingertips touch my face he growls.

"See?" I gesture to him with my eyes. "Promise you won't go in with me." She shakes her head, no. "Then at least tell them you don't know me."

"No," she says, "I won't let—"

A jolt and a squeal of tires throws me up against the back of the driver's seat. I fold, crying out, and slide down onto the dank floor, smearing blood down the Naugahyde of the seatback. As I struggle onto my knees, something sharp from the floorboard sticks to my palm. I grab for Terry and scramble up to regain the seat. I rise to see we're only stopped at a red light. A string of three patrol cars are crossing the intersection.

"Goddamn," the driver says back at our chaos.

"See?" I breathe out, wiping my blood from her cheeks and chin. "See?"

At the hospital Terry walks a fine line trying to explain how I ended up doing this much damage to myself, when she says with the same breath that we aren't very close friends.

"I swear, she's a friend from the base, that's it."

The nurses' jaw twitches when she asks, "You two aren't *friends*-friends?"

"Aaahhh, shit. No, just regular friends, look," Terry's voice lowers to a calmer tone. "She's bleeding here like all mad crazy, are you gonna do something about that or just keep asking me for a copy of some marriage license?"

"Yeah. Sure," the nurse nods. "Okay, what's her name?"

Softly, like it's the first time I've ever moved my tongue, I have to correct Terry on how she says my last name. She stutters, making it sound like Stanlon. My words come out like stepping on dried-out snail shells: brittle, supporting nothing.

"Scallion, Margarite Scallion, it's Scallion."

The admitting nurse pauses, surprised, and strains towards me to hear. They both glimpse the condition I'm in for just a second. Looking down at her papers the nurse sighs, but lets Terry off the hook, she's free to go. Me they keep.

In this bright room the nurse clears away all the blood from my hands and arms. She's taken away the washcloths and my bloody t-shirt and given me a dry hospital gown to wear, but she leaves the tears on my face. I'm crying again; feelings keep getting in the way of my thoughts. I need to think. It's hard.

A doctor comes in to see my wrists; he makes a point of not looking me in the eye. He asks the nurse for a shot to numb the area before he starts suturing.

As he sews me up he looks over my head to the nurse and tells her, "Guess who's preggers again? Your friend and mine, Nurse Weasel."

"God," the nurse answers. "What a cow she's gotten to be. How do the two of them even have sex?"

"Pretty gross, huh? And now a second little weasel on its way. Talk about a nauseating couple. They deserve each other."

"Boy, Greg, you were lucky to dump her when you

did." The nurse consoles him. "I always knew you were too good for her."

I look up at his face, curious to see him better. He's an average looking guy, on the short side, going bald. His nametag says Captain G. Caprio. I wonder how bad this Nurse Weasel could possibly look for him to hate her this way. Our eyes meet and he frowns. Then he pulls tight on the stitch he's just made, jerking my palm up towards him, like I'm a beggar. I look down, confused by the pain, then up at him again. He pulls roughly at another stitch. And I see something in his eyes.

I'm supposed to be inanimate. He's making me guilty of listening. He's mad at sounding so—what? Petty?

When my eyes continue to hold his stare he digs the needle deeper, showing who's boss. I can't hurt him like he's hurting me. But I know I need to stare straight into his eyes to let him see I have his number.

It costs me. When he releases my wrist white pressure points, like finger marks, standing witness to the sutures. With this hand I reach down into my boot for the razor blades. While the nurse is busy handing him another suture needle for my other wrist, I slip the blades into his white coat pocket. A present.

Here, I mouth, no sound at all, *a little something for your troubles.*

That first night, because of overcrowding on the woman's ward, there isn't any place to put me. I'm tagging after an orderly, weary. He's about to go on a break, he gripes out loud, "one more damned thing."

I follow from area to area as he searches for an empty bed here in the Psyche ward. It feels about two in the morning. We stop at the Nurse's station, and pointing at me the orderly asks.

"Where should this one go? There's no more room in B ward."

The nurse behind the desk glances up from her chart and shrugs. She reaches over the counter at the station, feeling with her hand for something back there, then comes up with a set of keys. She tosses them to my orderly, who motions me to follow again, this time down a new hallway we haven't explored yet.

"This'll do for the night."

The door he's unlocking has a plastic plaque on it—"ORDERLY'S DAY ROOM –♀" Underneath that someone's taped a hand lettered sign that says *Staph Only*. He doesn't flip the light on, just ushers me into the room, pointing to one of the beds. Light spilling in from the corridor shows someone already asleep in a second bed.

The pillow feels cool, cloudy, and the sheets are light and comfortable on my shoulder and thigh. I draw my knees up, making my body into a ball, wrapping myself around the stitches on my wrists. The clicking of his key in the door, and his steps receding down the hall, are the last things I hear before I fall off to sleep.

At dawn, a noise, *buzz-buzz, buzz... buzz-buzz,* tapping a code-like rhythm, wakes me and I uncoil from the crouch I've slept in, stretching out onto my back. Everything from the night before comes to me as I lay there, keeping my eyes shut to the faint morning light. The *buzz-buzz, buzz… buzz-buzz* continues. Someone at the Nurse's station must think there's somebody in here to wake for duty.

Then I remember the other bed over there, the woman asleep from last night. She sits up, groaning. I hear her mumble, "God, why do you trouble me so?"

Whoever's at the Nurse's station keeps up with the *buzz-buzz, buzz… buzz-buzz*. Maybe they're listening to music, I think, probably forgot she's in here.

There's a noise. Something's wrong. The woman's rushed my bedside. My eyes pop open in time to see her fist smash down onto my left eye. Bam! Bam! Bam! Three shots connect before I get my pillow over my face.

But she doesn't stop.

Strange lights flash in my eye with each blow. I'm counting the hits. Seven, eight. My voice is screaming; strong, I've never heard it like that before. It comes from somewhere outside of me, and as my pitch and volume grow so does the flashing behind my eyelids. Eleven.

The buzzing stops, I can hear feet flying down the hallway.

Fifteen.

Two frantic voices out in the hall are shouting.

Nineteen.

These are new voices, not the ones from the night before. *Why am I noticing that?*

Twenty.

Still screaming, I can hear doors opening up and down the hallway. Then someone's at this door, rattling the locked knob. Twenty-two.

All the while the woman remains standing over me. Silent. Pounding as I scream.

Twenty-five. No words. A frustrated grunting. And the sound of the blows with my screams. Feet outside have gone running away. Twenty-nine, thirty, thirty-one. Then the sound of keys rattling in the lock.

Thirty-five. Someone's back again.

Thirty-seven. *Shoosh*. The door's flung open, the light's clicked on.

Thirty Eight.

Like magic, the attack stops. Slowly, I take the pillow from my face to see this girl, dressed in pajamas like me, turning to confront the orderly who's not moved from the door. She stares at him, and holds her arms crossed high on her chest, making an impatient grunting sound, like he's bothering her.

"Carla, what are you doing?" the orderly demands, not stepping into the room, but leaning against the doorjamb. Carla retreats to her bed, sullen, still silent.

She gestures towards me and answers flatly, in a deep southern accent, "she is my heavenly torment here on earth."

"Right, I forgot about that." A bored voice. He waves for me to get out of bed, ordering as he turns his back on us. "C'mon. I'm off duty ten minutes ago; let's get someone to look at that face."

It's a big blackening bruise, from over the bridge of my nose, across my eye, and up my left temple, raccoon-like, like something that wasn't protected by a pillow at all, like she spent the whole time pounding right on me.

It was such a nice fluffy pillow when I first laid my head on it—you'd think it would have protected me more. I can't wear my glasses—it hurts that much. So I stay away from all the black girls on the ward—in case one of them is her—that Carla.

It feels like everyone is staring. One girl comes and sits near me but doesn't say anything. I wait for it. If she'd speak up, I think I'd be okay to answer her. She feels safe for some reason. But she just sits and sometimes she rocks. On and off she makes a low noise—I think she's growling. An orderly says, "Sheila, come get your meds," but she doesn't go—Sheila. I've heard them call her twice. I thought about asking for aspirin—for the pulling feeling the gauze on my stitches makes, but I really don't want to use my voice, or have anyone look me full in the face.

It seems to me there's two types of sailors in here: boys who've disconnected and guys who should be in the brig. Most of the brig guys are argumentative and threatening. Lots of cussing and spitting. The others, the boys, they're just lumps, not moving on their own, not getting out of the way when a brig guy goes off like a gunshot. Just lumps of green-wrapped boys.

There are lots of both types. I've spent most of the day watching—I think Sheila's mostly brig guy, with boy around her edges. I'm not sure how the others categorize me.

Sheila tries being my friend, in a sideways kind of way. We talk, small stuff, like "You reading that?" and "Can I sit here, too?" She's six-feet tall, if she's that short. Mostly she sits rocking. Or she stands and walks around, fast and purposeful, keeping her hands clenched, tense, tucked real tight under her arms. I think she may have cut herself too. She never goes when they call her for meds.

Someone laughs. It's Campbell, a shaggy boy: all wild eyes and thin, a problem on the ward. He stands over me, and Sheila starts cussing and pounding on the chair back she's leaning on. The orderly says real loud—not just to her, "Restraints, Sartori?" She goes white and yanks her hands back up under arms. Campbell's bony elbows and shoulder blades stick out at funny angles under his pajamas like they've been popped out of their sockets and never put back right.

I sit, shielding my black-eye with my free hand until Sheila comes and bumps at him with her hip, menacing. "Beat it, or I fuck you up bad, J.C." From the look he gives her that push must have hurt him plenty. He stiffens then moved away.

"Get mad at that freak!" Sheila urged. She sits down next to me. She understands me, and knows not to try to touch me. Sheila says, "It'll all be over soon," she tilts her head to the dark spooky lounge in general, "this'll all go away," she assures, determined.

I consider the dark ward, poor sad J.C, and Sheila—anger backed into a corner, this tough girl, crouched tight beside me, and I sigh to myself. *Sheila, this will never go away.*

J.C. must have squealed. Another orderly comes up to us and hauls Sheila up off the couch. "I warned you, Sartori." He's holding the cotton restraint, and trying to get one on Sheila's wrist. They struggle; it looks like she'll win, but only until three more of them surround her and the first orderly. They use a take-down move on her so she's pinned flat on the floor.

They cart her away like they're carrying a body-sized bushel basket between the four of them. They do what they want to us when they want. One of the brig guys mutters, "At least she'll get to lie down on her fuckin' bed."

I'm gritting my teeth now, but I want to punch someone right then. J.C slides back up pointing at my face, asking, "You did that to yourself?" *Idiot.*

I want to make someone bleed. Like Sheila said just before they took her away, I want to get mad. Raising my wrists, I push them up into his face, inches from his nose. He draws back like they're cobras, "I did this," I hiss. "The eye was a gift."

I push my chair out, bumping into J. C. I push past him and dart from the lounge. Behind me I can hear him politely introduce himself to some other patient, "Hello." His voice rising and breathless. "Have we spoken about your sins?"

I'm not sure how this brig guy got these babies but I'm gonna take them anyway. Group session's long over. The orderlies are off behind their station counters and this brig guy and I are sprawled on the couch in the day room, acting like we're watching the fuzzy-screened TV. There's a rumor some of us will be shipped somewhere first thing tomorrow morning, the scuttlebutt's flying around here like all mad crazy—but you can't go by any of it.

This brig guy isn't mean or scary like J.C. I mean, yeah,

he shakes a lot. But he might just be pissed off. And he's holding. He wants to wait out his discharge time in the brig. More opportunity for access, as he puts it. But they've got him in here instead. No one's talking about why that is, so Brig Guy just sits in sessions and kicks at peoples' chair legs. In the Day Room he slaps his trembling hand down hard on tabletops—maybe just to see if the catatonics'll jump. He was one of the ones staring, in the last session. When I cried.

Brig Guy says from the side of his mouth, "Garden variety opiates, of sorts, homemade—touch of codeine," as he drops two into my waiting palm, and smiles at some lady in a commercial, "first taste free for new customers."

But I really don't care one way or the other. Sheila's still in lockdown. All my fault and there's nothing I can do. After watching the way they took down Sheila, sitting through how Justin is still allowed to be as pervy as he wants, and no visit from Terry, I really need to self-medicate. Brig Guys' friend, Martin, whispers, "If it weren't for the smoke we'd get you stoned, little mama."

I wave him off. "No need." I say, swallowing dry, "this'll do." His face is all munched up too, like my eye.

"Yeah, it should." Martin asks, "What you weigh? Ninety-eight? A hundred?"

"One-oh-six."

Brig Guy gives me an appraising glance, muttering, "Yeah, sure, carrying your sea-bag on your back maybe." He tells Martin, "this won't take no time at all." Back to me, "What's your name?"

"Mimi." I tell him. Then I realize he probably meant my last name. We sit back and watch TV for real until I can feel it coming on. It doesn't take long.

Brig Guy checks my eyes, and pronounces to Martin, "Mimi El Stoner." Martin nods in agreement, affirmative.

I study Martin, his bumpy, lumpy cheekbone and cracked lip. I point, and quote from some novel I read in High School. "What was it a girl—or a midget?"

Martin and Brig Guy crack up at that. Brig Guy's grinning, "I like this chick," and I know the rest of the day will be okay, 'cause I don't cover my eyes, or cry at all, hearing him say that. And for the rest of the afternoon I almost don't think of Shelia at all.

Our plane stands, silver dipped in dust, reflecting sunlight. For the last half hour our military hop's been loading for take-off. The second couple of pills are wearing off. But not too fast, I took them on an almost empty stomach. Brig Guy slipped them to me this morning, "You're a very diverting chick," he tells me as I'm leaving.

The plane's glare flashes sunlight at our group as soon as we zombie-step down out of the gray Naval bus. There's twenty-five of us being sent up North, to a less acute Naval facility in Oakland.

Like the rest, I wait, wrapped in my green hospital pajamas, feeling some bewilderment, a bit of sorrow; I didn't get to see Sheila, didn't get to say bye.

If someone snapped our photo, I'd be the one who stood out from the other sailors; small and separate—the way your thumb does next to the rest of your fingers. My four-day-old black eye still draws looks. Gauze encircles both wrists. For once, my outsides are mirroring my insides. That we all wear the same green pajamas makes the line seem like a row of fun-house mirrors reflecting one broken person again and again.

How could this many broken people exist in all this sunshine without more noise? I wonder, *shouldn't I hear shattering glass?* I glance down. The sunshine bouncing off the tarmac shoots pain-arrows directly into my wet eyes, so I lower them and stare at my feet. My shadow's disappeared entirely. I close my eyes and raise my face to the sun, praying: *Please let time stop, so I'll stay invisible forever.* Hearing the sound of my whisper escaping my lips I flinch, and reach to wipe the wind-whipped curls from my forehead.

A dulled pain travels, like a lagged current, up from my wrists and into my brain. The dangling sleeves catch and pull at the sticky ends of the bandages, snaring and lifting the gauze from around my stitches. Everyone in line shuffles a few steps closer to the plane.

A breeze rising up from the flat expanse of asphalt circles, swirling around us. It's true I see it now, like Shelia says, "It'll all be over soon." The wind's snatching and yanking at me; it pushes me off my hesitant footsteps and roughly forward onto the plane.

On board, I watch through the tiny porthole as the others climb aboard. It's too much of a risk to make eye contact with the sailor to my right. All the seats on the plane face backwards, to the fuselage. Slowly the line of embarking sailors dwindles to only the bed-ridden and wheelchair-bound still on the ground waiting. They're wheeled backwards through the rear of the fuselage and secured against bulkheads with no more wasted motion from the orderlies than farmhands stacking cordwood. I draw my seatbelt taut across my hipbone; a piece of reality, like the stinging in my wrists.

"They're loading us backwards to confuse us," someone behind me says, "so we won't find our way back here. Goddamn fucking Navy."

On the tarmac, a new group of patients arrive. Just stepping down from another bus, they hold still and squint into the sun, too. I see Sheila. I touch the empty seat next to mine, *she could sit by me*. But she wavers there on the tarmac, those thin blue foam slippers dragging against rough asphalt. Something's wrong. Sheila's still restrained; white straps tying her arms to her sides. Her head lolls, slack. With each slowed step, her chin droops even more. My hand moves from her seat, back into my own lap. I cross my wrists, holding myself—bound—just like Sheila.

As I watch, the wind whips at her blue cotton robe, her constricted walk an embarrassment against the broad palm trees and sunshine of the airfield. Turning away, I pick nervously at the skin between my eyebrows. The smell of the surgical tape, strong in my nose, takes my attention. But a calm, clear thought brings my eyes back to the porthole; *She's not going to the same place I am*. The plane makes noises for take-off, but remains trembling on the ground for a long moment to taunt us further. The rumbles excite me; I feel more alert and risk a look around at the other patients. I can't; the faces shake me with their starkness. *I'm guilty*, I think to myself, *I'm not like Shelia at all. I'm gonna get better.*

To hide myself I concentrate on the view outside the plane, though I know—I'm guilty out there too.

Secrets of the Days and Nights

THAT CHRISTMAS WHEN I was still ten, there was more than just the big red book from Mr. St. John for me. Mama gave me a collection of the Brothers' Grimm Fairy Tales. And one big, shiny white book about myths for children, written by a guy whose last name was Kingsley. That was the best of the two, the myths.

Barbie got a sewing kit in a round blue basket, with a pin-cushion in the shape of a tomato. And a new pink brush-and-comb set. She wouldn't let me touch it. "For blonde hair only. DON'T even think about using it." Chance got a magician's cape with a top hat and a play wand. Mama was real good with presents when Christmas was around.

Mama invited Mr. St. John, our social worker, this Christmas. He also gave us a slim book for the whole family, called *The Prophet*. Mama was touched. You could see it in her face. My big brother Artie opened that gift up, after

Mama read the tag and handed it to him. We all reached for it but he held it up over our heads yelling, "Hold it! I'm doing this. *Pero, primero siéntense.* Siddown."

So all of us kids sat down in the wrappings and ribbons and then Artie went through the Table of Contents, reading the chapter titles and whose name Mr. St. John had written next to them. I felt very proud hearing Artie say my name, "On Self-Knowledge. Duffy," because then he turned to the page and read out from the chapter, "Your hearts know in silence the secrets of the days and the nights." Justine and Artie both nodded at that. They're the oldest of us five, so I figured that maybe later I'd ask them what it was supposed to mean.

Mama's chapter was 'Reason and Passion.' I found that out after, when I got to hold the book and flip through. Artie must have missed it, 'cause he hadn't read that out loud. The drawings were nice, kind of fluffy, but only in one color.

"Duffy. Coffee," Mama said, and I ran to the kitchen to put a pan of water on to boil. Coffee was one of my jobs. You have to use matches to get the burner going. And you have to be sure to blow out the match, then run it under water from the sink, and then you still can't just drop it into the trash. Just in case. So there's lots of steps. But most of the time I was good at it.

I ran back to our Christmas and Mr. St. John and Mama were on the sofa, laughing over something. Her eyes were bright, and I was glad it was a nice morning with nothing going wrong. Everybody was smiling. Chance kept granting wishes to the girls. "Wishes for ladies!" he called, tossing the cape back over one shoulder. "I got wishes for ladies here." The top-hat was too big for his five-year-old head, and only his ears kept it from falling onto his nose.

I scooped up *The Prophet* and brought it over to Mama. "Mama, here's you," I said, holding out the book to show her the chapter in the list.

While she was reading the title from my hands, Mr. St. John said, "You two have the nicest dark hair." Mama liked that compliment. With Mr. St. John just back from the Peace Corps she thought he'd be a good person for Artie to be around.

Mama said, "Let's see the chapter," and I flipped to it. Holding the book out like a waiter at a table with a steak on a plate. Like they do in the movies. She was still smiling at his hair praise, and I added, "But Mama's has the coppery red in it."

She couldn't have gotten too far in reading when she reached up and laid her hand on my shoulder; her thumb didn't move much, but the fingers, away from Mr. St. John's face, with her long red nails, they dug into the back of my shoulder. I straightened up. The burning was hard, but I didn't bend at the knees. Didn't cry out. I saw I'd done something wrong, maybe I showed off. So I closed the book and held it on the side she didn't have a grip on. I pulled the book away, unhurried, till it was behind my back. And still she didn't let go.

"Thank you, *m'hijita*," she said in a low voice. Then she released me and folded her hands in her lap, and looked back to Mr. St. John being nice to her.

"Annnny wish you want…" Chance cried out.

Barbie yelled from the kitchen, "The coffee water's boiled off again!" And then my knees did tremble. If Mama got mad then Christmas was ruined. But Justine jumped right up, saying, "I got it, Mama." And Mr. St. John, he stood up too, straight and tall like a hero, "I need some gum. Duff— want to walk with me to the corner store?" And like Cary Grant, he grabbed up his coat and me, and we stepped to the front door.

And just that fast I was outside and safe.

He didn't need me to get any gum, but I was glad for the rescue just the same. The Union Pacific train whistle sounded low and long a few blocks away and I thought of the hobos and the glue sniffers who hung around the tracks. Artie warned us about staying away from them. I figured if Mr. St. John could have a talk with them, maybe they'd all go join the Peace Corps too, so Chance and I could go and find bottles along the tracks to sell. That might make Mama happy; us helping out by bringing her a loaf of bread or a quarter worth of lunchmeat.

Coming out of the corner store Mr. St John walked on the outside of the curb, like I was a lady. I thought of something ladylike to say, because I wanted the Peace Corps stuff to rub off on me too. "Thank you for the book, Mr. St. John."

"Oh, you're welcome, Duff. I'm sure you're going to get a lot from it as time goes by." He smiled down at me from way up high. His sky-blue eyes were still strange to see, here in this neighborhood. Here we were all mostly Mexican. Even the other kids in my family, half-white—all but me.

They didn't have eyes as blue as that.

"Tell me something I don't know," I asked. It was a game we played whenever he visited. He was the only one who wasn't mad that I'd skipped two grades; that was something kids in East L.A. weren't supposed to do.

"Hummm. Look at your hand, Duff. You see these lines?" he asked, pointing to his own hand. "Here? This one and this one?"

I looked at mine. "Uh-huh."

"They're very important. That top one's your heart line. That one's your head line." He reached and ran his nail along that line and my fingers curled. I giggled. He went back to his own palm, "This last one, here's your life line, look, see how long and deep that one is? Know why?"

I looked at the deep brown line running off my palm and into my wrist. "'Cause I'm Mexican?"

"Close," he said. "It's because you've got an abundance of energy. You'll be very determined to reach any goal you're questing after."

"—like a lucky charm?" It was a really deep line.

"Sure. That line says you have what it takes to get anywhere you aspire to."

Like a lucky charm. Right there in my hand. I'd never drop it. And no one could come take it away.

"Can I ask you something, Mr. St. John?"

"Sure, Duff." We walked slow and it was nice to not be hurrying.

"When you said to reach any goal I'm questing after. You mean like Theseus and the Minotaur? Through a labyrinth?"

"Sure. That's right, like a quest. You accept this challenge and you'll be rewarded at the end."

"What challenge?" I asked.

"The one from your chapter in *The Prophet*, 'On Self-Knowledge'."

"What'll I get?"

"What do you want, Duff?"

I thought a moment while I concentrated on not stepping on any of the sidewalk cracks. My own quest. Boy.

"To be somebody," I decided.

"You are someone. You're Duffy Chavez. The girl with the lovely dark hair." He swung my arm all playful when he said it, and spun me back around like we were headed back to the store, but I stopped walking and got serious in my eyes, so he knew I wasn't goofing around. I needed to be clear. I wanted him to understand. I looked back behind me to my house and then real low I told him: "No, I mean to BE somebody, to not be invisible."

"Ah." He nodded. "Well, yes. I believe that's a fitting reward."

He didn't make us start walking on again. He put his hand on my shoulder. It really hurt from when Mama had grabbed me.

I waited, for the special words of the Challenge; like in the myths. But he was looking far off down our street. Way beyond the brown of Mama's front door. And finally I asked, "If I accept your challenge can I have that as a prize? Can I end up being somebody?" I looked up into his face.

"Yes, honey," he said. "With self-knowledge you can definitely be somebody."

"Should I kneel or something?"

He smiled down at me. "No, this is 1965. The New Frontier and all. Very advanced. How about we shake on it?" And he took his hand from my shoulder and held it out to me. I liked it better on my shoulder. Even through the hurt.

"Okay. Mr. St. John. I accept this challenge." I shook his hand real hard.

The next morning, after Christmas, when the rest of the house was sleeping, I opened up the Writer's book he'd given me and on that inside page I wrote: "Duffy Pilar Chavez, Age 11, 1966." Even though it was still 1965, and I was going to stay 10 until July came again. And even though my nickname, Duffy, was my sister's way of saying DeFoe when we'd been babies. Either one's a silly name for a girl to have, anyway.

It was the beginning of January when we heard the news that Mama had found us a new house and we couldn't stay here on Hockert Street any more. She told us over dinner. All five of us at the table and her at the kitchen doorway, standing like she was getting ready to run if we took the news badly. Artie and Justine and Barbie, all blonde and older than me; Chance, the baby, and blonde too. Then me, just Duffy, and as jet-black of hair and the brownest eyes you could get. All waiting for Mama to say more.

She'd made us flank steak tacos with all the toppings in pretty little colored bowls, set out up and down the table, and a big casserole dish of Spanish rice, and some zucchini with melted jack cheese on it for the vegetable. And we had red Kool-Aid, too; Chance's favorite dinner. Mama always made what he liked best, her baby boy. Although Artie, being the oldest of us all, was the champion of eating the most tacos.

"It's a bigger place, a nicer neighborhood." Mama's cough broke into her words, "no trains." She covered her mouth with the crook of her elbow, then breathed in big to keep talking, "—an' I think it's a good move." None of us answered. Mama reached up with the heel of her palm, cigarette pointed up to the ceiling between two fingers, and wiped back a curl off her forehead.

Because Justine was the oldest girl I figured she'd be the first to say something. But no one spoke up. Barbie started in softly tapping the table leg with her foot, till each tap grew into a kick, her blonde bangs jumping. *Tick, tick, tock, tock, whap, whap,* the noise went, till her short pageboy haircut was doing the same jumps around her ears, the noise growing from mild to mean. Justine let out a breath, and Chance asked if anyone was going to eat that last taco.

I reached over to put it on his plate. Justine finally said, "Okay Mama, we'll start packing after dinner." Mama took another drag from her cigarette, ran her finger around the top of her cup, started to say one more thing, then stopped herself. She turned and left us to eat.

After dinner we walked back into the living room and Artie asked if we should take all our stuff or not. Mama frowned at us, a strange look in her eyes—like she'd been fooled by the question. "Of course. We're not leaving anything. Pack it all."

But she might've been lying, and we needed to know for

real. The Foster Homes were still in our minds and she really didn't see what a brave thing it was for Artie to step up and ask.

Mr. St. John, he didn't come the next day with the others to take us away in separate black cars. Like those times before. That was the part I hated the most, seeing Justine kneeling and looking back at me while I did the same from a car going the other way. Me alone in another car riding farther and farther away from the rest.

Mama wasn't fooling; we really were moving—all of us—to a newer, bigger house; she was taking all of us with her. Even me. The one who got Mama mad all the time. Sometimes, I thought if we were Indian that would be what the tribe would call me: The Mad-Getter.

When we had just moved back in with Mama she would blow up sometimes. Like a sudden monster you forgot to think about in a TV show. Then she'd line us all up for a punishment—even when only one of us had done something wrong. Like playing so hard something would get broke. "Which one of you idiots is going to be first?" she'd ask.

And I'd always wait a breath; send a word from my mind to the guilty one. But they never moved from the line. So then I'd step forward. Just to be done with it. She hated me doing it that way. Maybe it made her feel bad that we were all idiots all the time. Maybe it was that she liked, really liked, to fight. And I failed her. 'Cause she would get madder and yell, "Dammit—fight with me." But I couldn't.

So we packed the house up. And we didn't complain or whine, like I think Mama thought we would. She kept walking from room to room, looking in at us with something like confusion in her eyes. With me, when our eyes met and we stayed that way for a moment, there was that disappointed look—then she just turned away and I didn't look again.

Mama told us we just needed a truck for the boxes and the washing machine. The furniture was being moved for us. She was nervous when the furniture company came and took all the beds and chests and lamps and the sofa and chairs.

But we'd been moved lots of times before, and this was nothing new. Like Artie always joked, we'd been born into captivity. She was the only one who wasn't used to it. Her and Chance.

The morning after the guys in the 1st Street Furniture truck took everything. Mama yelled, "Duffy, come get these milk bottles!" I'd just been thinking how great it was that the store we got the sofa and beds from was kind enough to move our stuff to the next house too, their store's jingle circling and circling under my breath.

We were eating breakfast off the counters in the kitchen and Mama waited for me at the front door. She wasn't in a good mood. She'd been fighting with Justine all morning, there was nowhere to sit, and now she was starting in on Artie. She slammed the front door closed as I came near, and she walked back into the kitchen. Yelling more.

I pulled two half-gallon bottles from the wood and metal milk crate, and walked back to the kitchen with them each pulling on my arm sockets.

"What's this gonna cost me, buster?" she was asking Artie. She'd set to work on making the lunches. Five of them. The boys got a full baloney and cheese sandwich and a full peanut butter-and-jelly one, too. Us girls got the lunchmeat and cheese, but only a half of the peanut butter and jelly. Chance was standing on an old milk crate at the counter, waiting to drop in the apples, one to each lunch bag. The voice on the radio sang '*Trece treinta! K-W-K-W!*' and then the man said, "Ahora, más."

On the last trip through the living room with the milk bottles my fingers gave out, and one of the bottles slipped from my grip and shattered on the wood floor. I froze but couldn't stop myself; I started crying, thinking of the beating that was coming next.

She came out and held the other kids back with her outstretched arm, "Artie get a mop. Chance stay out of here, you're barefoot."

I looked up at her; she looked like she wanted to cry, too. "It's okay. Just stand still," and she wasn't mad.

I'd been trying so hard. She reached in and plucked me from the flood and she kept repeating "It's okay. Only milk. Don't cry." And while Artie mopped and swept up the glass, she leaned against the wall and slid down to sitting with me in her arms, against the wall and out of the huge milk puddle. She held me and the surviving bottle in her lap, and stroked my hair, and softly, in Spanish, she kept saying, "*No estoy enojada.*" *I'm not mad.*

That night before the moving day we spent sleeping on the

floor, using clothes and sheets to make lumpy pallets. I told Chance that this was how cowboys slept—out on the range, under the stars. The blue shadows of the empty room and the boxes piled high, like far-off mesas, helped the story as I whispered it to him. "The cowboys, they get to sing to the cattle, low and soft 'cause it's night and they don't want to wake up any coyotes."

I went on and on about cacti and rattlers and the moon on the hills in the distance, till I could hear his breathing slowing down for sleep. I rolled over and scrunched even closer to him to keep warm. He lifted his head and whispered in my ear, "Duffy, can we be cowboys when we get big?"

"I thought you wanted to dance on the TV."

"Can't we do both?"

Me and Chance, we sat in the back of a truck. It was the kind with the wooden fences stuck into the sides. All our things from this house were around us, and there we sat, stuffed in-between the boxes and the washing machine. Artie whistled as he tied a tarp over us, wrapping the ropes tight against the truck's fence sides; turning the sky into a circus tent. The girls, Barbie and Justine, were up in the cab next to Mama, and then Artie got to driving—tall behind the wheel, even though he was only just past fifteen by a month or two.

The streets slipped past behind us; I watched them go from out the back of the truck slats. The liquor store Mama sent me running to, to get her cigarettes. The Amigos' Burger where she'd meet us after work each payday, to treat us to hot dogs and soda, all of us each getting to choose anything we wanted from the menu board. It was all getting away—the school, the playground. All of it.

I tried to make each place a story in my brain. Something to hold and remember for my New Year journal. Something to retell Chance late at night. Something saved, because Artie was going to be on the freeway soon headed someplace only he and Mama knew how to get to, going so fast I knew we'd never see any of this again.

"Once, on Hockert Street, I met Mama for the first time," I told Chance. "I was little, as small as you are now."

He hunched his shoulders down and leaned his head in close, to hear me over the rush of the freeway noise. "Were you in kinnergarden like me?"

"No, I got to skip that, you gonna listen? Well, Mama, she was the most beautifulest lady I'd ever seen up close. Like a movie star. Like Sophia Loren."

Chance added, "An' she wore a red dress with a big shiny black leather belt."

"And big, black, round earrings, too," I said. "There on the front porch, with the four of us waiting and inside a baby was crying. She took me aside and told me, 'If you're good and you help me with all the others, I'll let you in and you can stay.'"

"An' you peeked in the door to see the noise and saw me asleep, barely a baby, and that's why you're my guardian angel." He nodded. This was one of the "How I Met You" stories I'd told Chance over and over again. He knew most of them by heart. You have to do that coming from Foster Homes. No one else knows if I cried as a baby, or if I was sweet or good, no one ever will. I wanted for Chance to have things different. And from now on I'd have to add the Hockert Street stories to them, too.

The freeway's wind was rushing over our curved backs now. Keeping us low, wrapped into ourselves, a punishment. And then it came to me all at once, the secret of the days and nights. A new place wasn't just new to who moved there. Me and Chance, we were gonna be new too. The back of my neck tingled with the thought and suddenly that freeway wind wasn't hurting me anymore, it was washing all the whole of my life away. Cleaning me up to any new person I wanted to be once we got to whatever new street Mama had picked out for us. I could pick out the best of me and only be that. I could win the challenge and never drop a bottle of milk again in my whole new life. I could teach Chance to do the same.

I turned my head to his ear and raised my voice loud over the smell of gas and the noise of the tires rolling by us out the sides of the flapping tarp.

"Once, when we were locked out and it was getting dark, and Mama was still at her job, Artie and Justine were nowhere to be found—"

"An' my stomach was hurting cause I was hungry—" Chance added.

"—an' I found a big box and stood on it, I lifted you up on my shoulders, up against the house. Even though your feet wobbled, and you were a-scared and shaking, you were brave. You crawled in the little window up over the bunk beds in the back room. You let us in and saved the day." I never told Chance the part about me not wanting to jump up on the box and climb through the window myself with him below watching: a-scared to do it because he'd see under my dress, that I had dirty underwears on and maybe he'd laugh at me. I was new now; I could change my stories like I wanted. My underwear secret I'd save for the journal.

Chance grinned down into his knees, remembering how he'd saved the day. "We ate the rice from the refrig-alater."

So, I said, "And the moral is, even the smallest have gifts to share."

Scheherazade's Little Sister

I KNOW I'M dying.

And I'm not trying to hold onto life—I'm trying to hold onto living. Listening to Stevie's stories kept me waiting for the next day. I wanted more time, and I wanted Stevie. Not to mother her, or take her to raise. It was more than that. Her stories did something. I felt I'd be able to let go if I could just glimpse life the way she'd seen it. Just once. One last story before I left.

That first time I saw her sitting on her red jacket out in front of Leo's shop, a tool and die place next to mine, I knew then. This wispy girl; that afternoon she held court making all the fellas gathered around slap their knees and elbow each other, laughing as she told her stories.

I thought she was some high school senior there to help Daisy, Leo's wife, with front office bookkeeping. But I found out later she was a machinist, working the screw-machines, doing lathe work, drill press. Second operation stuff. None too wispy.

The sun was warm, so my guys and I stood out front, burning a few. Actually the guys did the smoking. I just stood strategically downwind, feeling nostalgic.

The laughter from her circle floated to us, grabbing my ear, the liveliness in her voice drawing me in. I thought about joining her, but stopped myself.

Small industrial parks are like small towns, everybody knows everyone's business. I hated how the guys changed since the chemo started in on me. How my standing with the smokers made them mope and twitch; the sad way they shifted away from me. And the guys who depressed me even more, some refusing eye contact, softer voices, asking if they could get me something from the lunch wagon, if I needed anything done.

Like I was suddenly their old grandma. I hated that. My needs were no one's business. I listened a moment longer, grinned at Jeff, then walked back into the dimness of my shop, all the way back, to sit as far from that laughter as possible.

The shop's no great shakes of a business itself; we sub-contract for bigger firms. Just a small link in the chain: assembling bulletin boards, cork, chalkboard, and the white. But it kept me in Coronas and dope during my chemotherapy, and it paid my fellas, Bobby and Jeffrey; and Jeff's little sister, Candy, an under-the-table wage, which at the moment, was as far ahead as I wanted to think.

This girl-next-door always lugged her ox-blood leather jacket around with her, never saw her without it, like a trademark, either slung over her shoulder, or like that day out front, stuffed under her butt for a pillow. Useful jacket. Maybe she thought she was a rebel, I don't know. Anyway, she caught my eye often, and not just because of her jacket.

It was April when I first noticed how she'd come hauling into the parking lot, looking like a cross between a pixie and a pirate. I wondered why her folks let her work full time, why they didn't want her in school. But then, some kids are out on their own going into high school. At least she wasn't up on Sunset, homeless and selling it for a place to spend the night, whatever her story might be.

On rare mornings her boyfriend pulled into the parking lot and I could see the two of them in a clinch in his shiny blue truck. Doing everything to each other *except*, well, you know. A real weak-looking kid I thought; too bony, pale.

"Must be some college kid," I mentioned to Candy, "bet his dad bought him that truck."

Candy laughed so hard soda sprayed out her nose. "Ellie, you crack me up."

It seemed who I thought was the boyfriend was actually a *girlfriend*. Ah, well. In the parking lot first thing in the morning, her scooting out of the truck, her step a little lighter than usual, she'd saunter over to Leo's shop.

Of course word got around about the girlfriend, but still I was drawn to her. After a while I looked forward to the mornings; I'd sit scrunched down low in the front seat of my MG and stall opening my shop, so I could watch her coming around the corner. That red jacket dangling off her shoulder, stepping the way she did. Jaunty and light. Strange how it mattered; to catch a glimpse each morning.

Thanks to some brain-dead Accounts Payable clerk at my distributor's main office, one week in July I was stuck short with the payroll and I had to pay Candy with a bag of my medicinal Thai Stick. Candy, in turn, ended up becoming friends with this girl over a minor dope deal. Candy called her Stevie. I found out she'd just turned twenty the weekend before. I'd never have guessed, she seemed so small. And her pale girlfriend with the blue truck was a college student, living at home.

In my shop Stevie confided stuff to Candy during their lunch breaks. Sometimes personal stuff, but always light, the way she'd tell it. Like she was skimming on top of the hard times, like nothing was so bad it couldn't be funny. While she and Candy yakked on to each other in the back part of the shop, right behind my partitioned office space, I'd sit; quiet, listening through the thin shop dividers. She was living with a group of kids, in a five bedroom house, out by Redondo Beach.

"... see, we get this guy's duffel bag and we layer ice, beer, ice, beer, steaks, ice, beer, then take the van, head out to the pier." I sat imagining her out on the sand in the rain, playing football. "Then David, that wimp... We could've hurt him bad, but we just tossed him into the surf... We were soaked."

She held down a second part-time job, evenings after work. "It's not like I have anything else to do," she told Candy, "you haven't seen the truck around...we broke up. Her dad threatened to take it back, so I'm history. Me, I'd have held out for a Mustang before I said *adiós*." I leaned forward in my chair, to get closer. "It's no big deal. I've been on my own since fifteen. Not like I haven't been dumped before."

"That's the best part about repeating the same mistakes in life over and over again; at least you're sure when to wince."

Maybe hearing that is what changed things. She said she hitched to work most mornings, even when it rained for most of March. I almost gave myself away, laughing out loud at one of her stories. How could I not? More and more I wanted to know her.

That's when I started to think *maybe I could give her a ride in the mornings. She could work as my house-girl; drive me home from the next round of chemo. If she drives stick. I can pay her with my MG when I kick off. No hitching anymore.* I wondered; was I hooked? It felt lonely, but good and hopeful at the same time. I felt a tingle when I thought about her and those stories; how I could make them mine.

After that smoke deal, the girls sat in my shop during lunch breaks all the time and usually they'd be smoking a joint. No problem on Candy's end. Not much harm comes putting boards into boxes and shipping them. But I worried when Stevie took a hit. Being a machinist, the way those cutting tools came at your fingers was scary enough without my dope added to the equation. But she'd stop at one hit, waving the joint away, smiling *no more* through her teeth, like the First Lady, gracious, declining a second cup of tea.

Early most weekends I'd see her boss, Leo, in the wet parking lot while we unlocked our shops. Every once in a while we'd stand shooting the bull and after a while I'd manage to get the talk around to his guys, Stevie in particular.

"She's an alright kid,", he said "isn't afraid of lifting twelve foot bars, brass or steel, stocking the lathe or screw machines."

"Some girls can."

"Man, I swear." He shook his head, "these dammed machines are eating my guy's fingers for lunch."

"Finger-burritos," I nodded. Those cutting tools. He'd already lost two machinists to worker's comp, one his own sister-in-law.

"But not Stevie, she's the only one still with the tips of her fingers."

For some reason, I felt proud to hear this bit of info. Like she was already mine; the glory reflecting on me.

He said, "Hell, If she weren't a girl I'd be paying her fourteen per, like I do Joseph, as it is I'm giving her a raise to seven-fifty soon."

I knew this Joseph from around, a real dick of a guy. Didn't know his ass from an Allen wrench. Why should Stevie get shorted? That's when I decided. What could I do to maneuver her away? Leo was about to give her a raise. It wasn't like Stevie was a flake, or a thief, or worse. A coughing fit shook me, then it hit; I knew Leo and Daisy were death on drugs of any kind and the whole complex knew Candy smoked my dope.

"Good thing she's got all those fingers, considering the time she spends with Candy at lunch," I said, shaking my head and looking down at my key ring. Letting it sink in. Leo caught on; his face going through the pros and cons of it. I knew I started something big, and I needed it to go my way.

Late, maybe after six the next Friday, I walked into my shop. Candy, Jeff, Bobby, and Stevie all sat around my office, looking real pissed off. Then I remembered; *oh, shit, they know I was talking to Leo.* Candy was enraged. I froze. Nauseous like after Chemo.

"Do you know what that Leo just did?" Candy asked, "He laid Stevie off today."

"He what?" Would they notice me sweating? "What for?"

"Said it was between me and Joseph. Said one had to go and Joseph's got a family. So it's me."

"What a dick," Jeff said. "What a shit."

"Yeah." Bobby nodded.

Everyone was fuming at Leo. I wanted to jump in and save the day. Say come work for me. Say I'd pay her more than seven-fifty, that I'd leave her my MG. But I was afraid, I kept quiet.

"I know I'm only an old dinosaur, but how's about I fix us all dinner and we try to figure out a new job for Stevie?" Big smiles lit up all around. My dinners being wonderful stories in their own way. Jeff hopped off a stool to go turn out the shop lights. And we all stepped out into the cool of the evening. Later it dawned on me that my fellas were usually gone from the shop by four-thirty at the latest. Pulling strings, yep.

We considered piling into Jeff's little red Honda, but with Candy's 10-speed folded up in the back, it nearly became origami on wheels until I suggested my MG.

I prayed Stevie would ride with me. "C'mon," I groused, "you can't *bend* the old and infirm this way, especially when they're buying dinner." Inside I chanted like a Buddhist, *Please, please, please.* I breathed again when Stevie spoke up.

"Yeah, I'll ride with you. Let's not bend dinner."

Were my hands even gripping the wheel during the drive? I couldn't say. We stopped for groceries. My guys roamed the aisles, hungrier than usual, so we ended up splurging on dinner fixings. Stevie's eyes were as wide as a birthday-girl's seeing the backyard with a piñata, clown, *and* pony. I got such a kick out of her discretely looking away from the total up on the register.

Back in the car I said, "Sorry you lost the job."

"Don't worry. Jobs always come up to me and say, 'Hey you, c'mere.'"

I caught a glance of myself in my rear view mirror, smiling far too much. She looked over and smiled too. "Candy says you tell, ah, you know, a lot of—" I felt foolish, like a voice-cracked high schooler. I cleared my throat, "—says you're pretty funny with your stories."

"I could probably make you laugh."

"Nice. I could use one. Or two."

"You're gonna be dying, huh? Candy told me."

Strange to have such a young voice say that out loud. The words still stuck in my own mouth.

"Yeah." The pain in my chest spread. "You said it." I didn't turn to see her face.

"You need someone to take care of you." She didn't ask, just said the words.

My hands grew damp, then weak. They slid on the

wheel. "I'd give you anything you need."

Stevie nodded in the dark.

After the dinner we sat and lay around the living room, too stoned to do more than sit and look out over the deck at the sun kissing the ocean. From the floor, Jeff groaned and rolled over, knocking his head on the leg of the coffee table. Candy broke up into high, tippling giggles.

Stevie got up from the couch and started browsing the room. Candy followed, pointing stuff out: my sister's pen sketch of me at seventeen, over the fireplace. The ancient reel-to-reel, the piano. My lungs started in. A sharp shooting, right down along the scar tissue from the last time: breathing wasn't fun. I inhaled a numbing toke from the joint I held. No help.

Bobby started to snore softly from the floor. Shifting my gaze down to watch him, I tried to keep the tight look around my eyes to myself. The girls dug up a movie they asked to play, "Nah, we'll sack out if I turn down the lights. Let's play word games instead."

At this Jeff nudged Bobby awake and Candy clapped her hands and scooted back from the bookshelves to sit on the floor. "Yeah."

"What word game?" Stevie asked, trailing behind, surprised at everyone so suddenly awake.

"You'll love this," Candy said, "it's always different, Ellie makes them up."

"Once we played *That's The Way The Cookie Crumbles,*" Bobby yawned, "I came up with *That's the way her back porch swings.*"

Jeff added, "but the best was "*Grossest Thought of The Week.*"

They all laughed and I took the lead. "Okay, tonight I'll make it easy for Stevie, we only have to tell a story." They all leaned in to hear. "Let's make it about the worst thing you've ever done to someone. But it's got to be *amusing.*"

Stevie paused to take another hit before continuing.

"…So there I was, upstairs in the bathroom. This old queen is downstairs yelling for everybody to get out of his god-dammed house."

A high giggle burst out of me. She shot me look and grinned.

"And his *false teeth* were just *sitting* there on the sink. So I thought to myself, 'Well, *hell!* Why not?'" Her voice rose, innocent, but nothing covered the mischief in her eyes.

Tears ran down Candy's cheeks and Jeff shook so hard I was sure he'd wet himself. I coughed, wiping my eyes. The boys bumped foreheads laughing and Candy broke up even more as they tried choosing to hold their skulls or sides. We all clapped and stomped, we had our winner.

"Oh. That was great, that was heaven!" I held my hand to my chest to keep from a bad fit.

Candy looked over at me, "Ellie!" Just that quick, my fellas were up on their feet surrounding me.

"I'm okay," I waved Jeff away, "just gimme some water." When the water came and I could breathe again, I told them, "Honest guys."

The reel-to-reel ended and I pointed at the slap-slap-slap noise it made, "Get that, Bobby, would you?" I wheezed.

It was then I noticed Stevie holding my hand. She wasn't looking worried like the others. Her look said, *I know about you. I'm not afraid. Don't you be either.* Our eye contact felt like maybe she'd handle the scary, can't get my breathing right parts of being around me as much as the part about the free MG.

But I looked away. For the fear of getting it all right at last. Our eyes met again. Stevie smiling down at me, me repeating, "I'm okay now, really."

I tried my best. The Saturday after that dinner, I helped her move her stuff to my house from her place at the beach. Two boxes, that's all.

"I've kept it pretty drab I guess." We stood in the doorway of my guest room. So common. I was ashamed to bring this bright girl here. The beige walls and tan coverlet on the bed made me want to cry.

Stevie looked around and sat on the bed, "It's okay, no problem."

But the longer I stood there the more I wanted to fix it. Make it better, "I didn't realize I wasn't ready for company."

"Really, Ellie, I don't need anything more." She tried to make herself look at home. But in the blandness, in her red jacket, she sat like a rose in the sand.

"Well, just for the room then, just to liven it up. Now with—now—I think." Stevie smiled, watching me stammering. But I got brave. "Well, we should hit the mall, no? Put some color back into this place."

"Okay then," she agreed, "to the mall." That nod. My blush must have matched her jacket. In the car I talked all the way; I had plans. We'd be happy.

For a while I thought we were. Late in the day, before dusk we'd sit in the living room, for the sunset. Each time I'd ask for a story. I didn't see the problem until it was too late. That time she said, "Another bit of my life?"

That day, the sun was still up as we settled back for the show. Stevie draped her jacket on the back of my chair and sat. At dinner I'd given her a gift, a pen and a hard-bound journal. Something for all her stories. The pen was the best one I could find, gold and red, with a strong solid stroke to it. I'd tied up the pen with a maroon ribbon, almost the color of her jacket, and wrapped the journal with fine red rice paper embossed with golden suns and moons.

My hands trembled as I handed it to her.

I thought she'd be pleased, but when I asked for another story she changed the subject. "Who drew you there?" She pointed above the fireplace.

"The line drawing? My sister. When I was a few years younger than you are now. How do you like me?"

She studied it. "I've never seen you that way, only this way—the way you are now."

My voice dropped, distant to my ears. "I'd rather be anything than the way I am now." I tapped the journal on her knees, hinting for a story. "How about you? Anything you'd go back to?"

Her fingers smoothed the rumpled wrapping paper next to her on the couch. "No. I'm going forward, far as I can get. The past is just stories I tell."

"I love those stories." I stretched my arms over my head;

leaning back I felt the taffeta of her jacket lining. Like rose petals. Like home. "All of them. As many as you've got. Me, I'd give anything to—" I leaned forward. I might've reached out.

Maybe she could save me, if I could only hold on a bit more. "Can't you give me your stories? Be my Scheherazade?"

Stevie hid her hands away, stared down at the pen in her lap. "Ellie, who do you think I am?" I trembled hearing her ask. She held up the pen for me to see. "I tell stories to show myself I exist. I make them funny because the real thing never was."

She frowned and held out the pen, leaving her palm open until I had to take it. "And I tweak the endings because I have hope." She set the journal down on my side table. "But I'm no Scheherazade. I'm not even her little sister."

I looked up, willing to beg. She said, "My stories won't keep death away." Her eyes closed, like she thought I'd never understand, like I didn't know my own dread.

She was crying, looking around the living room for something. I looked too, though I wasn't sure what she needed or that I could find it for her. I started crying too, because then I knew. I picked up her red jacket, feeling the taffeta lining for the last time. Dusky roses and a faint jasmine scent. I handed it to her and she walked out of my living room, the front door closing behind her with a crack.

I sat, still holding the red and gold pen. The next time I raised my eyes, the sun sat low on the water and shadows hung over the walls. In the dimness I couldn't see my sister's sketch. Without looking, I felt for the switch on the lamp at my side, my arm brushing Stevie's journal. I clicked on the light.

A small, gold circle warmed the room. Reaching for her book of blank pages, I flipped through all the emptiness that could've held the times and places she'd said couldn't belong to me. Until I came to the last page, I wanted to write *But, I need you.* I breathed in—a torn breath.

Something broke inside. The pen was moving in my hand. I watched my tears falling on the words I'd set down instead.

I know I'm dying.

Clichés from the Barrio

*I*N THE DREAMS *Mr. Arreaga, the old baker, acted like he didn't hear the cracking sound in Raymond's chest, like cartilage snapping.*

Raymond, who has a nice white-collar job working on his computer from home, fights the dreams by refusing to lie down and sleep. But he only ends up with insomnia. This time he hasn't slept well for more than a week. At first it was just a matter of wishing his wife and daughter good-night at 11:00 p.m. and then not turning off his computer monitor until a few '*Raymond, GO to BED*' reminder messages snaked across the screen. Then he found himself startled at 4:00 a.m. in the morning by the clanging of his neighbor's iron security door as the guy left for his shift at the bottling plant.

But now it's 7:00 a.m. and Raymond finds he's still up, wishing his family a good-morning. He trails after his groggy wife while she occupies herself with her morning routine:

brushing her hair with rough, angry strokes, removing herself from his presence as often as Raymond reaches for her, ignoring him as she searches through the flat basket on their coffee table. "What did your cat do with my keys, Ray?"

He asks if she's going to eat breakfast. She holds up a miniature bag, her lunch, in silent response. His pale daughter can only mumble "Still up, Dad?" on her way to the bathroom, where she'll spend nearly an hour arranging her hair for school.

"When?" Mr. Arreaga asked in the dreams, his floured hands trembling as he wiped them on his grayed apron, leaning his elbows on the counter in an arthritic position of prayer.

Ever since Raymond turned the corner—up all night, awake at sunrise—he's made an approximate note of the time when the glow through the living room blinds seems complete. The sun has been up since about 6:58. He gauges the insistence of the traffic's flow outside his window. When it grows louder and eclipses the low volume of his desk radio, Raymond tries to work. But the dreams and the baker's voice repeat in his mind.

"November twenty-second," Raymond explains. "Heroin."

Shaking his head at the belated news of loss, Mr. Arreaga murmurs, "Ay, Dios, such a waste, such a sadness, a year ago today?"

It is then that the pain in Raymond's chest explodes and takes him to his knees right there in the little panadería. Raymond's hot eyes blur the breads laid out in the baker's display case until he can only see his older brother, Frankie, laid out in his coffin.

"You didn't hear?" He asks the baker again, this time in a flat new, logical voice. "I thought you knew."

"No," Mr. Arreaga answers. "No, if anyone would've known it would be Sylvia—she never said."

In his living room Raymond touches his chest to be certain things feel normal. He does his best to push the voices from his mind, kissing the top of his daughter's head as he hands her lunch money. Raymond nods to himself and tries to realign his vision. He closes the front door on the day.

The baker acts like he did not hear the cracking sound in Raymond's chest.

He wanders from his desk, tucked into the corner of the living room, to his bedroom. The trip doesn't require many steps. The duplex is a 2 bed, 1 bath affair, with unadorned window and doorway sills, a flat roof that holds onto the cold and heat, and a communal backyard the size of a boxing ring. He notices the covers on his bed are not tugged to one side. No expectant space for his late night or pre-dawn return.

There was a time when he first found her, and she was new to his insomnia, when Raymond's wife would wake in the middle of the night and gently coax him back to bed. The cat was still a kitten, sleeping on their headboard; one gray paw dangling in the air over their heads. That was when their duplex had just the right feel to it. Raymond would lie there in the dark, his eyes open, his wife's body pinned against his ribcage, the mingled scent of shampoo from her blonde hair and sharp sweat from his pillowcase in his nose.

But now his dreams are so bad that he cries and jerks, often waking with little starts that scare the cat. And his wife. He pictures her at work and fears she confides to friends during lunch breaks, that she's glad for his insomnia; more room in their double bed alone.

The pillows look inviting, but the thought of lying down and closing his eyes brings that heavy pain to his chest, lodged just under his sternum. He returns to the relative safety of the living room and his computer.

In his dreams he tries not to, but he has to ask after the baker's oldest daughter, Sylvia.

Frankie's first girlfriend, back twenty years or so, years before this duplex. Sylvia Arreaga—from second grade to that night on the freeway—Raymond secretly hated her, loved her then hated her all over again. She had taken Frankie from him, in the end, taken him twice. But in between she also gave Raymond a taste of real family, a taste, while living with his still wifeless father and Frankie, which Raymond had nearly forgotten.

When Frankie first noticed Sylvia and her younger sister Beatrice walking past his father's house, Frankie sent Raymond racing to get the pretty girl's name.

"It's probably something stupid like Irene or Sylvia," Frankie yelled as Raymond took off from their porch. Raymond ran after the girls and tried to look down at the sidewalk at the same time so as not to step on the unlucky square of cement, the square Frankie pointed to the day of their mother's funeral, three years earlier. The square with the worn stamp that could not be read—proof that it was bad luck.

In Raymond's nightmares all the squares on the sidewalk are cracked open, by roots the size of arms and legs, every square marked with that worn bad luck stamp. He runs and runs, but he can't stop himself from stepping on all the bad luck.

With his family gone, Raymond slips his feet into his stiff tennis shoes and steps outside to turn on the sprinklers. He waves to his neighbor on his right; a slim, wasting woman, who stands at the curb holding her grand-daughter. With the baby's little fist the woman waves goodbye to her daughter who's headed off. The baby wails as her mommy drives away. His neighbor turns her back on the street and heads indoors; the baby's wailing continues. Raymond turns his back to the cries and pretends to study his lawn, this sorry patch of sometimes green.

He can see being six, walking home through Calvary Cemetery from The Boulevard, a downtown theater. Frankie, bigger and older, trying to scare Raymond while they walked through the tranquil green and the long shade of headstones. Outside the cemetery Frankie hugging Raymond. Making a dash across the wide street, coming up to a freeway overpass; a perfect place for the two boys to practice spitting, as the sun makes its way down behind the tall buildings of the Los Angeles skyline. City Hall stands farther west, beyond their horizon, like one raised concrete finger, a warning in the growing dark.

On the way home Frankie points to a huge billboard of a blonde, smiling from the passenger seat of a red car, and says: *That's what mom looked like.* And because Frankie was twelve years old and never wrong, Raymond believed in spite of really knowing better, that his dead mother was blonde and drove a big red car.

In his yard, Raymond notices the pathway had worn away across the edge of his lawn, serious enough to bare some of the roots of the pine. He knows that next Saturday his wife will tell him this damage is his fault. During the week she is blind to the subtle ways their rented home slips into disrepair. It's usually dark after work when she parks her car in the alley carport behind the duplex. But Saturday is soon enough to be held accountable for things he has no control over; the things he cannot save, yet cannot close his eyes to.

In his old neighborhood, Mr. Arreaga's daughter Sylvia evolved, broadened her speech so no one would mistake her for the fourth generation Angelina she was. She worked hard for two years. After school programs for kids from the Ramona Gardens Projects, summers as a Junior camp counselor for the National Conference of Christians and Jews and, in the end, earning herself a scholarship to Pepperdine University, with all the white people, out in Malibu. Frankie, and Raymond, waited behind.

Then Frankie tested in the 98th percentile on his ASVAB scores in his senior year, so he signed up for the military when the recruiter told him he qualified for Avionics Electronics A-school.

His father laughed at the words *ASVAB*, and *A-school*, took a long pull from his beer can, and said, "Go, go live with the paddys, talk like a scientist, 'Join the Navy'—all that shit." But when Frankie showed up at the building where the physicals were given and the final enlistment papers were signed, the Navy talked him into an open billet as a Pharmacist's mate, in Utah. Raymond, six years younger, had finished high school a year and a half early, spending his time doing nothing, still looking for that blonde in the red car.

Today, with Frankie gone a year now, Raymond tries his hardest not to remember more. Keeps his eyes open whenever possible. Forgetting how the Arreaga's let Frankie sleep on their couch when he was fourteen, and the boys' whole world was a war with their still wifeless father. Raymond hasn't even driven through the old neighborhood in fourteen years. *I was twenty-six* he keys into his computer, and the pain expands in his chest. *Don't cry*, he thinks, *do anything, but don't cry. You run or you fight*, Frankie used to say, *pick either one, but do* something, *Ray.*

Raymond just wants this pain to go away; he wants to stop moving and to have his mind slow down for half a second. Instead, he stands and heads to the kitchen. While he pours from a plastic pitcher, his cat tries to crawl into the fridge. She voices loud, aggrieved meows when he holds the door closed. So he relents, and sprinkles some grated jack cheese into her food bowl. It'll keep her coat shiny, he rationalizes, as if his wife is standing there criticizing. Or is that eggs with dogs?

You run or you fight.

Raymond gathers his keys and jacket. Aside from the

gritting of his teeth, the rest of his body's gone numb. Leaving the duplex, he heads toward his old neighborhood. He reaches Garfield Avenue and turns north. He drives. He wonders what made him take the streets instead of going east and jumping on the freeway. He fiddles with the radio, trying to find something familiar, something he knows. First he passes the two casinos in Bell, then Garfield turns into Eastern Avenue at the bend near Bandini.

Frankie's voice returns; a young Frankie, just out of the service, driving his blue Impala, his attention on the thin joint he's rolling in his lap. He steers with his thighs, taking quick peeks up at the road as his hands work quick and sure above the shoe box lid on his lap, a box lid full of pills; reds and black beauties, they roll around in the weed. Frankie licks the rolling paper to seal the pinner he's made.

"Ray," Frankie grins, as he swallows a quick swig of Dos Equis, "it probably passed you by, but Garfield just turned into Eastern, and at Telegraph, it'll turn into Atlantic, and up on Huntington Drive, it'll change again to Los Robles. Every street turns into something new. All the streets meet somewhere, and all of them can take you home—if you're not careful." Then Frankie laughs that stoned laugh of his.

Singing along with Jimi Hendrix on the radio, he twists the steering wheel left and right then left again and grins, "This is an uncontrolled intersection, Ray, so we drive uncontrollably."

Long after the intersection the Impala still sways and bounces from the worn shocks. It was then that the first crack, as thin as spider's silk, began in Raymond's chest.

Raymond drives west on Olympic; up ahead he sees

Sloan's Dry Cleaners. Seeing the faded slogan *in by 12 out by 4,* soothes his mind, until he turns right onto Eastern Avenue. The cemetery is there on his left, edging the freeway. Raymond keeps his eyes on the road, refusing to see, the way he refused to see most of Frankie's problems, even refusing Frankie's funeral last year. But Frankie's voice is calling him: '*Hey Ray,*' that stoned laugh again, '*Hey man, When you gonna visit?*' The laughter grows louder; Raymond tries to ignore it. The tightening of his chest burns, so like Frankie said, he does something about it and steps down hard on the gas.

Past Third Street, soon he's at Brooklyn Avenue, except now it's been renamed Caesar Chavez Avenue (how long ago did that happen?). Raymond drives slowly on the alias street, looking for the joke that reminds him of Frankie and Sylvia in good times—a little taco stand with the pink neon sign; *LUPE's #2.* But the stand isn't there anymore. He turns and circles the block, retracing the ride back four streets, starting at Eastern again, to be sure. It's gone. Raymond can't even figure out where it might have stood. Car horns honk behind him. He picks up his speed, continuing west, reassuring himself that at the corner of Fresno, no, maybe it's Evergreen, he'll park and walk into the Arreaga's *panadería* for some *pan dulce.*

The neighborhood's scenery, as the streets slip past his windshield, no longer feels nostalgic or recognizable. Raymond's eyes view them the way a white guy's would, noticing only the clichés from the barrio that outsiders would notice: hand-painted signs in Spanish he can't read, skinny dogs following behind stooped old men. The words from the Mexican music, blaring from corner markets, understandable only in his heart, not to his ears or tongue. *At least the panadería will be there,* he tells himself.

Townsend Avenue, Ditman Avenue, Bernal, Concord, then Fresno. But there's no sign for *Arreaga's—Family Owned* or *Breads and Pastries for All Occasions.* No storefront window full of *pan dulce* trays. Raymond has reached Evergreen now, and he must stop and park as the sudden sobs shake him, bringing the hot shame of tears in daylight to the back of his neck, the depths of his chest. He parks in the sun and cries.

The last time he spoke to Frankie, Raymond was twenty-six. Sylvia sat waiting for the two of them on a freeway shoulder for four hours when her Vega broke down in Pasadena. As the sun went down, Frankie lost them more and more time trying to find her. Retracing twisting streets, they were hopelessly lost up near Sunland, three cities too high above the problem. Raymond, who still didn't have a license yet, knew he should have been the one to go into the liquor store for directions. But Frankie insisted. "Got it covered."

After waiting fifteen minutes in the strange parking lot, staring at the white-washed bricks of the liquor store wall, Raymond steps out of the van. He finds Frankie squatting on the curb in front of the store with a circle of drunks, and a six-pack of beers between his feet, five cans already emptied. He introduces the drunks to Raymond like they're old friends.

It takes a full twenty minutes to get him back into his van and on the road again. Dusk is settling before Frankie finally comes stumbling toward Sylvia out of the growing darkness with no tow truck following, but with a triumphant grin and two black bottles of champagne, one in each fist, from the liquor store.

In the sunshine Raymond still sits in his car, his eyes are no longer wet, closed. The tune on the radio is one he thinks he remembers. He sees that the sun is higher now, but he doesn't roll down the windows; the warmth that he has trapped feels good on his skin; all that's missing is the smell of bread. Raymond sets the driver's seat back till it's nearly horizontal. The pain in his chest has gone, he can breathe, but the breath he takes in is a ragged one. Raymond closes his eyes again.

Sylvia looked to the van, her eyes meeting Raymond's; the look cut through him like none of Frankie's drinking managed to all evening. Then she turned, shook her head, just once. In the van's headlights she yanked herself from Frankie's sloppy embrace, throwing up her hands, sobbing, not trying to stop her tears. Raymond sat doubled over in the shadows of the van. He swallowed the sounds of Sylvia's crying, until the back of his neck and the center of his chest felt like they were trying to reach for each other to meet somewhere in the middle. He knew he'd break right in two. Frankie fumbled under the hood of the stalled car, managed only to lose two sockets, dropping them from an unfamiliar wrench handle into the depths of the engine. Raymond remembers the shame of Sylvia's tears most, and the sound of clattering metal on the asphalt in the dark.

When the tow finally came and followed Frankie's

weaving van off of the freeway, Frankie ended up leading it the wrong way down a one way street; trying to get to Los Robles. *Which should lead to Atlantic*, he promised Sylvia, *and on to Eastern*, he said patting at the air, reaching back between the van's front seats for Raymond.

Later Raymond always told that night's story in the best light. Making it funny, mixing in word for word Frankie's speech about all the streets being one. But here, where the *panadería* isn't, Raymond sees that that night was the first time he heard the cracking sound in his chest. And the last time he remembered listening to Frankie.

Raymond starts up his engine to head back home now, away from these memories and back to his suburb duplex. He finds a different bakery and comes away with a big white bag. Then he finds the first freeway entrance he can and points his car onto it, not bothering to take the streets home.

In his head he practices telling his wife about Mr. Arreaga, there in his shop. He'll make it funny. And light. Yeah. He runs the story through his head over and over; how happy the baker was, handing Raymond a warm empanada, full of pumpkin; Raymond's favorite. Raymond practices the forged words that will make the telling a happy one; how the baker nodded with Raymond's satisfied smile. How he handed Raymond a warm white bag full of sweet breads, and in a benediction waved away Raymond's dollars. Raymond won't mention thinking to ask after Sylvia. And maybe not about the baker coming from behind his counter for a hug, even though he can see it there, as clear as day, bigger than life in front of his eyes. That will be just for him.

Raymond smiles, thinking of telling his daughter about LUPE's #2. In his mind he can almost hear Mr. Arreaga saying, "Take care, Ray. You look like you could use some rest."

"Yeah," Raymond says to his windshield. "Yeah."

Anna Calling

WHEN WE WERE both fifteen, Anna stood in the center of Pious X Girl's Senior High quad, smiled, winked, and started yelling. Out came every cuss word that she knew or could make up for the occasion. Loud and clear so nuns for miles would hear, even the ones working at St. Linus' on the next street over.

Uniformed girls began gathering, snickering, then laughing out loud, as they threw nervous glances over their green-sweatered shoulders to the cafeteria door. I couldn't bring myself to match her volume, let alone the blaspheming, so I stood next to her and shouted the Act of Contrition up to heaven. I figured the nuns wouldn't be too happy about me choosing a prayer, any prayer, as my half of Anna's lunchtime duet.

"Goddammed fucking venal pit—" Anna called out.

I winced, piping in, "—heartily sorry for having offended—"

"To hell with all you Jesus-sucking pieces of—"

"—detest all my sins, because—"

"And Mary too, you shits!"

"—who art all good and deserving—"

"—Non-profit, my Christ-sore-ass."

"—to sin no more, and avoid—"

Sister Euphemia shot out of the cafeteria, more a 280 lb. bouncer fixing to break heads than an outraged nun come to silence our obviously non-God-fearing mouths.

My dad came up to get me from the school's bile-green offices and we walked home through the quiet neighborhood without a word. Then we sat, just sat, in the living room. I watched the shadows on the carpet inch across the floor until they waited at his feet, then kissed darkly at his toes. Like I supposed he was waiting, expecting me to.

When my brother Pete got home from St. Anthony's and dinner wasn't on the table yet, he looked from Dad's face to mine, "What's up?" he asked.

Dad pushed himself out of his chair and, looking past my ear into the air behind me, just said "No TV, no phone. No Anna. No argument." Then he climbed the stairs, back to bed, till he had to get up for his graveyard shift at the hospital.

My suspension lasted three weeks, and included painting over all the graffiti on the auditorium, inside walls and out. Not to mention the staggering number of rosaries I had to say. The nuns invited Anna to find another Sr. High to go to the devil at.

I tried staying away from Anna. Tried to believe, as the nuns had hinted, that she wasn't normal. All I wanted from life was normalcy; a father with a day job and a wife, a brother who kept to his own room after the 11 o'clock news. I coveted a calm voyage through my life and a best friend I could trade clothes with, preferably someone with taste. Secretly, I worried it was my coveting that was the root of my failure in receiving.

Anna told me she was drawn to me because I needed saving. She said it was like she was a siren, a mermaid on a rock. And she'd found me, weary, treading against choppy waves, and it was her job to grab hold and pull till I was on land. I've got to admit the part I liked best was when I was out of the waves but not yet on the ground, when all there was to feel was Anna's hand holding mine and my feet in the air. That was the best thing about Anna; even when, over the years, maybe our roles of fisherman and fish got exchanged more than a little bit.

Then yesterday, five days before my twenty-seventh birthday, Anna called. To say she was sorry. At first I missed that word completely. I only made out someone speaking in a vaguely familiar, softly feminine voice. A voice that sounded like—maybe there could be a relation, but not one I knew well. This voice had gotten maybe five rushed sentences into whatever script she was reading from when I figured *this is long enough to be polite to a telemarketer*. But then one of her words finally shone a light. And all at once, in a palpable way I realized—*It's her*. It's Anna calling. After all these years, she's calling me.

Anna, my savior. Anna who watched me for weeks in my freshman year at Pious X, and then came up, pointing her sinful red fingernail and said, "I'm gonna walk you home after school today. We're gonna be best friends. You got that?" I nodded, never questioning. And she did, and we were, from then on.

"Jeanette," Anna was saying now in my ear, "I'm calling to apologize. I'm sorry for that time in the quad, and for the baby kittens; what I made you deal with out back of your dad's house. And for the time my grandpa's plumbing went haywire, and I hid in his pantry, till I could face the situation—", she said "—and handle it."

Handle it, I thought, nearly hanging up then, *handle it?*

After the old man suffered his first stroke, Anna got ten dollars from her Uncle Frankie every time she spent her weekends with her grandfather. His house was so depressing; an old run-down place, peeling battleship-grey paint and smelling of mold, of giving up. It was always at least 20 degrees colder than it could've been, like he was practicing for the grave. The curtains in the parlor hadn't been drawn since her grandmother's wake, seven years earlier. The kitchen light was burnt out and the old man, Howard, refused to keep any real food in the musty refrigerator, just six-packs of beer. Out of the window above the spidery sink, you could see pale, bone-colored weeds, armpit high, covering his backyard, inching their way up towards his bedroom window.

The first time Anna ever kissed me was in his pantry. We were drinking our fifth beer—Anna's fourth, while I was still working on my first. She reached for my face through a hazy beam of light and pulled me toward her. I giggled, ducking out of her reach. All she said was, "Please."

"Get outta here," I slapped at her hand, reaching there in the sunlight.

"Please."

"Why should I? Huh, Why?" I was still mad at her from the last time with her granddad, and the plumbing mess.

"Because I'm asking." She touched the side of my face, soft. "Because it's me asking, me—Anna."

Anna, my downfall.

But I didn't have any words for her then, 'cause what I didn't hear was an apology for what she *didn't* do, for what she couldn't handle. She didn't say she's sorry that *I* was the one her deaf old granddad shot dirty looks at; the one who got the cussing, when all I was trying to do was get the old man to lift his dammed feet out of the toilet water that was running everywhere. She didn't apologize for the omissions. But then to be fair, she never asks for my apology either.

But she does apologize for the 'breakage' to my heart. Where do some girls get words like that? I wanted to add 'What about the theft of my soul, Anna?', but I didn't intrude into her monologue. There was plenty that both of us promised to keep silent about; lives that can never be redeemed, like those kittens; still life in a sack.

By June, senior year, the dark circles under my eyes couldn't be hidden anymore. I began losing weight. Anna asked questions. After I confessed about the nightly asthma attacks and that first time; waking to find Pete standing over me, one hand clamped over my mouth, the other down the front of his PJ's, there was no stopping her. That whole summer she begged my dad to let her stay over, night after night. Slandering her family and hinting at gruesome stories about her home life to convince him. How was he to know she was just changing the name of the rapist for my benefit? So she stayed over, my guardian angel, sleeping each night with her arms around me, like I was really hers.

First Anna tried telling Pete off, then threatened him, finally bringing beers and joints to share till he'd pass out in the hall, and we'd have to drag him up to his own room, all the while his hands grabbed, sloppy and insistent on her ass as we dumped him into his bed. And she took it all; anything to keep Pete from coming back to my room. Anna was the shield I hid behind, my mask of no worries. And I used her to make things feel normal, light. At first what I had to trade for it was replacing the beers swiped from her granddad's fridge and the packs of cigs stolen out of my dad's bedroom. But nobody gets it easy forever.

Labor Day. Pete and his buddy Vince got their own bottles, Southern Comfort, and after a summer spent drinking, Pete could hold his liquor now. We could hear them up in his room, yelling above the volume of Pete's stereo, banging and bouncing around, now that dad had left for work. Then the noise stopped.

Anna and I waited, not looking at each other; just waited. As soon as we heard them in the upstairs hall, Anna kneeled on my bed and pushed open my window, "C'mon, out."

"Anna, I'm not going out there."

"Yes, go, Jen, now." She shoved me out the window. When I landed my ankle twisted on something soft and wobbly in the high grass, then it went out from under me in a sharp, weird-heated way. There was a quiet noise, a small sound, then silence. I crouched down into the weedy pitch black and grabbed for my ankle. Above me Pete and Anna's voices floated out over my head.

"Where's the Princess, Anna?"

"Pete, get the fuck outta here. You guys're drunk."

"C'mon, Annie. 'Fess up. She under your sweater?"

"—get away!"

"We're jus' looking for some fun—"

"Pete!"

"—right, Vince? Les' all be buddies here, huh?"

The pain shooting up my leg made me nauseous. But I couldn't stand, even knowing she needed my help. I tried balancing there in the grass, to steady myself first, both hands on the ground. That's when I touched them; the soft shapes of baby kittens. I'd fallen on two kittens. They were both limp but still warm. In the dark I brought each tiny body up to my ear to check. But I had killed them both.

Above me, something had changed. Anna's voice was gone. The boys had quieted down too. I held the little bits of warm in my lap and cried as Vince said, low and excited, "Me next, man. Me next."

The next day we didn't say much. I wrapped my ankle and cleaned my room. Anna found a sack and a trowel in her Grandpa's shed. We buried the kittens under my bedroom window. She said a good-bye prayer, like that laid everything else to rest with the tiny balls of soft fur.

So here, with her voice in my ear, I wondered: an apology, who really owes who? I think about Anna at seventeen, teasing me. "Be careful what you wish for, lady. You just might get it."

"I'm serious," I giggled, "What good is Pete for? I'd trade him for you any day. I can beat *you* in a fight."

She grabbed at me; "You wanna fight? Huh? Do you?" But I twisted away, laughing, out of her reach, nearly falling into my mirror stand in my bedroom. "C'mere, I'll fight 'cha." She was grinning, her arms circling mine now from behind, pinning herself up against me, her breath at my ear. "Loser gives what the winner wants," she murmured.

I felt goosebumps rise on my arms. Did she know she was repeating Pete's line? To me—like this? I froze. I leaned back into her hold, thawing, sinking into it. *This is Anna* I told myself, forgetting about how she knew that line. This fight wasn't for real anyways, I told myself.

By nineteen the fights were for real. Anna strung out, Anna on our couch, the one my dad gave us when we found the little single to share by that park, after graduation. We had both changed so much in such a small time; me, refusing loans to her when she'd taken three hundred dollars of my college savings for the dope she'd gotten from Pete.

Anna moaning, "Please, Jen—please, babe?"

"You can fight this, Anna. I know you can." I wanted to touch her, hold her, but couldn't. Her skin was so dry that her tears never glistened any more. They disappeared as they fell.

"I'll ask Pete to front me. Is that what you want?" She turned from me to light a cigarette.

"You wouldn't do that. I know you."

"You've got me confused," she told the couch-back, facing away from me. "Take another look. It's me. Anna."

The tears started falling. And without me even feeling it start, I was crying too.

"Think about the good times, Anna. Like that first time, our time up in your room. Think of something good. Like you told me, those colored lights falling into the lake at the park, like neon rain."

She kept her face to the upholstery.

Then she turned her head towards me, whispering, "You don't get it, do you, Jen? Shutting stuff down isn't a selective thing. Babe—all that's gone." She breathed out cigarette smoke, her voice raspy, hard suddenly. "And I'm sorry here, but I'm only asking for fifty bucks to see me till morning."

In the end—here on the phone—she doesn't apologize for my one thousand, seven hundred and ninety-two dollars college money. She doesn't mention all those summers working at the old folks' residence for it; my Wednesday and Friday school nights, working Bingo for the Sisters at Holy Name. Or the life I said goodbye to when I found she'd stolen it, bit by bit. No word about the tracks and bruises on her arms and the backs of her legs or the puke I washed off her body, how many times after I signed her up for rehab? After she gave me her word, then going back to Pete to start it up all over again, I nearly remind her of all that there on the phone.

She pauses on the line. Like she can sense all I'm not saying. I think, *maybe she's gotten to the end of her list of sorrys*. So I wait, and then she adds, "See, Jeanette, I heard my phone ring, just one ring. But then no one was on the line. It's stupid, I don't know why, but I thought it was you. That's why I called. No game playing. I just felt it was you, so... so I'm taking it—as, as a sign, and so—"

I don't let her say it. I hang up before Anna gets those four words out. Whether they were going to be *I still love you* or *Jeanette, I need money*. Either way, I hang up. Then I take the phone off the hook before any more *breakage* occurs.

It'll probably be awhile till I can breathe right again, and I know it's stupid, but I actually find myself smiling as I think about her call. I put the receiver back on its hook and I sit, grinning at this one shining thought: Anna still thinks about me, so much that a ringing phone means *Jeanette* to her. I can almost take the apologies then. Take them to hold in my heart, close and—boy, this sounds lame, but close and healing. Like it was Anna there in my heart, back when we were—

How can I explain?

Well, you know, I guess—I just—felt like that first night with her, like I'd been rescued again. I felt glad. So that's why I put the receiver back on its cradle.

I'd gone one step from the phone, and it rang again. I was still smiling. I picked up, listening, in a high mood, till my brother Pete's words sank in. Like a rock, shattering my spine. He was saying "—line's been busy, Jen. Guess what? Guess who I got off the phone with 'bout an hour ago? Guess who it was, Jeanette? You'll *never* guess, never. We talked a good long time, too. Hah! It was Anna calling. Remember? Crazy Anna? She said her phone rang, just once, and she's not sure why, but—"

Going to Emergency

WHAT RIKKI REMEMBERS is jumping up off the couch for a Diet Cherry Pepsi as the commercial started. That and a wobble-feeling that strobed behind her eyes, just before the TV's volume rose up to a crashing level and she dropped like a corpse onto the rough carpet, face first.

The walls shook from the *BAM* of her contact. For a slip of a girl, 103 lbs max, she made a big noise going down. A full four minutes passed before Sheppard flushed the toilet and found her, still out cold; the commercials done with and the TV news going full blast again about another body found in the Ramparts District.

If it wasn't for the fact that her glasses had cut her cheek open, Sheppard might not have gone for their neighbor at all. "I'm okay, really," Rikki promised, pushing herself to the edge of his couch and balancing there with her palms. She felt the wood through the batting of the cushions under her slight thighs. "Man, that was strange," she repeated as she tried to hold her head immobile, like it was a crystal vase she was carrying around for someone who knew how clumsy she really was.

Sheppard opened their front door, leaned right and pounded on Number 12's place with a frantic, pissed off hammering that bounced back into their apartment, making Rikki squint and raise her shoulders to her ears. Luckily for Sheppard, Number 12's boyfriend, Tim; the gay guy they always saw running down the stairs at weird hours, was sitting on Number 12's barstool; shoveling down spoonfuls of Wheaties. A quick consultation showed Tim was the only one of them with a running car. "Sure. I can carry her, no prob."

Back in their place Sheppard, hanging there on the far end of the couch, made it clear over Rikki's hunched shoulders; "No. Just her. I don't do hospitals. Just her."

Tim murmured *umm-hum* and jangled his keys. Rikki couldn't lift her head so she worked at studying how his feet moved. Hypnotic; left heel, right toe, left heel, right toe, before Tim sighed and shifted into action, "C'mon, honey. Auntie T's gonna take us for a ride-ride. Up you go, now." Rikki didn't remember if Sheppard asked if she had her key.

"I'm okay, really," she apologized to the attending clerk. The clerk stole a glance at Rikki's cut cheek, licked her lips and followed that with a malignant look at Tim, who stuck his head in the window and emphasized *neighbor*, with a thin finger to his own chest, explaining the situation a bit more fully. Fully enough that they kept Rikki, and put her up on a high bed. Bending her legs to crawl up there nearly killed her. They made Tim go wait in Chairs, but he sneaked back to where they wedged her and waggled his fingers, trying for eye-contact, some sign of recognition. "Hey, Babe, I gotta go. My shift starts at eleven." Rikki nodded, then stopped. Dumb idea. She lay her head back on the cool of the sheet just before she passed out again, that crystal vase finally slipping from her hold.

It was a long night of waiting. A guy on the bed next to her sat in handcuffs. Rikki focused on his wrists, shining silver between his knees, but she couldn't lift her eyes to see his face. A Cop guarded him, his black thick shoes hardly shifting at all. Moving her eyes left and right brought on tears and she hated how they got soaked up by the gauze, stinging what was under it like all mad crazy. So all Rikki could tell about the Handcuff guy was that his voice seemed pretty benign. The only thing that passed between him and the Cop was a bored Q and A for the time. Rikki heard the cop answer at odd moments. 12:19. Going on two. 3:44.

Morning was nearby. But at 4:30 Rikki still couldn't raise her eyes very high. The pain. She'd heard several moving chins claim that there was nothing on the x-rays, nothing organic. X-rays were what Handcuff guy and his Cop were waiting their turn for.

Somewhere along the line someone mentioned *spinal tap*, but not till at least 6:47 a.m or so. She wanted to say, *Thank you for the time, Handcuff guy*, but it hurt her jaw to even think about saying yes or no. Even nodding hurt.

Rikki remembered catching a glimpse of the weird shoes Handcuff guy wore as he finally got his chance to slip off his bed and walk ahead of the Cop to X-Ray. They looked like mad shoes. Ones that always got what they wanted. *Ah, Rikki, cut the crap,* Sheppard's voice said behind her eyes, chasing the thought away. *Shoes don't do that, people do that.* But still, she thought, those shoes didn't look like the soft voice she'd heard all night. The tech they followed was telling the Cop he'd have to remove the cuffs in the X-Ray room and wait outside the door unless he wanted to get zapped. His choice.

Minutes passed before her tech with the spinal tap stuff came by. He did his damndest but he still poked her again and again before getting it right. Rikki was numb; she felt the pressure of the stabs but no pain. And she felt guilty that this guy was having such a hard time doing whatever it was he needed to do back there. She always felt that way with Sheppard. And Jimmy before him, and her stepdad Ray. It was always her fault. Her fault she was clumsy, never paid attention.

What was it in her blood? What made it take so long to work with? What was in her bones that kept mute and stubborn? Why couldn't they speak up and tell someone what the hell was the matter here?

The tech drew the needle back at last. His disappointment felt louder in her ears than the swish of the curtain around her high bed, or the groan from somewhere off to her left. *What is it you want?* Rikki asked in her head. Not to the tech, he was gone. She got brave for a second, whispering into her sheet, *"I wanna know why it's always my fault."* But that was just too stupid to even be a thought and so she gave up, closing her eyes for a while after that. Handcuff guy and his Cop never came back.

"I'm okay, really," Rikki breathed out slowly. She pushed herself to the edge of the high bed, feeling like a baby again. It took some doing, but Rikki was proud when she dangled her feet. She sat with her head dipped from the exertion.

"Whoa!" There came a flutter of thick white shoes, no one had moved that fast all night. "Honey you just had a puncture!"

Four or five, Rikki thought.

"You gotta lay still, dammit."

But—no one had told her to keep still. It wasn't her fault this time. No one said *you gotta lay still.* Like no one had even said she had to stay.

Rikki laid back down under heavy hands that wouldn't let her do anything else and then, once the fluorescent lights stopped throbbing, she whispered "Fuck this," and steeled her entire body to try and sit up again.

They were all pissed off at her and it showed in every voice that came at her, but Rikki didn't give a shit anymore. She was done now; done being here, and no one was going to stop her from going. Of course, this was LA County Emergency, so no one did.

She made her way along after signing the AMA form, her fingers keeping contact with the hand railing, her steps slow and deliberate. The bus to take her back to La Brea and

Coliseum was three, maybe four, transfers away. She'd have to hit up someone for the fare. But she had all the time she needed; no one was waiting on her. Rikki had the day to herself.

Halfway down to Marengo Street a nurse was coming up the opposite way, slow and heavy, a roll to her gait that said too many shifts in too few days. She stopped. "You okay, hon?" Rikki pulled back from the hand that looked like it wanted to steady her.

"I'm okay, really." She shifted left, bending; a stray cat refusing to be touched, though it cost her. Shooting pain rode some bullet train, headed south, down to her toes. Rikki felt her blood bubbling and coughing at the nape of her neck, her body shuddering, like Shep's last dead car; no compression. "Wait." Rikki kept her head down. Her voice came out like a puff of exhaust. "Do you have any bus fare?"

"Sure, hon." The blonde pulled four ones from her uniform pocket then let Rikki go on down the incline.

At the westbound 79 stop on Marengo, headed for Downtown, a guy waited in green scrubs. He was the only one. It was pretty early. As Rikki wobbled closer she saw his shoes and thought, *Nah. It can't be.* To test her sanity she asked for the time. It was. It was Handcuff guy.

He rubbed his shoulder like it hurt a lot, shifting and testing it, his shadow doing one half of a chicken dance on the sidewalk. Rikki acted like she'd never heard him before.

He said, "Don," to her quietly.

"I'm Rikki." It seemed weird but Don said they were both headed the same way.

On the 76 bus, rolling away from the sunrise, just inside of downtown, Don tapped Rikki's shoulder over her seat, then in a quick move slipped in past her to the window seat, laying both hands palm up on his thighs. "Hi again."

She'd just popped the 4th of the 15 Darvocets they shoved at her when she refused to be hustled back onto the bed. The irritated tech had told her, "Take one a day. You don't weigh enough to handle any more." But this was Rikki's pain. She'd downed those few dry, but her head and neck still felt present and accounted for.

Rikki felt Don watching her, aware for a second of it coming through the thinness of her eyelids, like the morning sun. What did he want? She hated being responsible for folks who were kind. Her eyes were still closed when she felt him peel the gauze from her cheek, familiar, easy, like he'd been touching her his whole life. She didn't even draw away.

"I'm okay, really," she said, with her eyes still closed; trying for other words. "But it's like…" pushing her bangs from her forehead, she added, "Like…like…"

"Like," Don echoed. Rikki's eyes flew open at something in the tone. A whiff of Sheppard; of Ray, of ducking too late. If her neck didn't hurt so much she would have winced.

"It's a pause word," she exhaled. And, "sorry," she added.

"A pause," Don enunciated, "where no sound should be." Rikki breathed through her mouth; she couldn't smell it as much that way, that familiar scent.

Man, that was strange, Rikki thought when that whiff faded a bit. Don carefully folded the gauze and tucked the ends of tape into a smaller and smaller square, the square neatly disappearing in his hands, magician's hands, not a trace. She held her breath to reach past him and rang the bell to transfer to the Wilshire bus. She was deliberate on the steps heading down to the sidewalk.

On the number 720 Wilshire, headed west for Santa Monica, Don's smile was gallant, though Rikki couldn't see high enough to look in his eyes, so maybe it was just her memory of his voice back at County. "Be right back," he whispered, patting her knee and swaying his way down the aisle to go ask the driver something. Rikki saw how brave he was with the riders. It hurt to watch, but she couldn't turn away. She'd never weave her way through folks, undetectable, like that. Don's hands politely touching the backs of the morning rush hour passengers, leaning in to beg a path without hurting his shoulder. No one gave him a sour look for crowding them. The bus was jammed. Rikki watched as Don leaned and balanced, turned and balanced, making his way back to her now as the bus rumbled and jerked.

He reached up with his good arm, holding onto the bar overhead, swinging slightly, a grin in his voice, very satisfied. "You hungry?" He let go of the bar to reach for her and pulled her to her feet in slow motion, all the weight on his forearm; Rikki felt like she'd been led onto a dance floor. "Sure you are. Let's get something at Cantor's Deli." And just like that they were off the bus at Fairfax Avenue.

In a booth at Cantor's Don explained, while not explaining, his exit from County. He'd 'fessed up to seeing her in Emergency. "*No cuffs, see? 'Cause metal Fu—screw's with the X-Ray equipment, right? Cop waiting on the other side of the door. Don jiggles on the table to screw up the X-ray. Gotta have a take two, right?*" He grinned. Rikki began to nod out just a bit, but pulled herself back into his tale, "*Tech says don't get up yet…be right back.*" Don chuckled, a sound like those shoes of his. His nice voice overriding the chuckle, he kept on with his tale. "*Cop's back to the door? Making a play for some short Filipina nurse's aide? …And humm, yeah. These scrubs just might be my size. Hmm another door…where's this lead?*"

He stopped. Studied his menu and Rikki over the top of it, then stated, "You're too pale. Lemonade for you. Good for retaining iron." He waved the waitress over, "One with your brunch and one to go, no ice. Looks like you need it bad."

No one had ever bought her lemonade before, for iron or not. She thought about Sheppard's '*Just her*' and Tim's '*Not me*'; the spinal tap and leaving Emergency. Rikki fingered out another two Darvocets from her stash, washing them down with the tartness of the lemonade.

And then Don did the weirdest thing on the table top. He pulled wallets from the pockets of his borrowed scrubs. "It's wonderful, the things you can get away with when no one's paying attention to their belongings."

Rikki just sat and watched as Don transferred cash and

cards to a single pile and slight-of-handed the important parts back into his green pockets. The emptied wallets he made disappear into the seams of the booth's Naugahyde seat. She heard, "Drink up". At least his hands gestured that across the table top. But Rikki couldn't be totally sure she also heard, *I loves me some inattentive folks*. She was waiting for a burst of maroon paper flowers next.

"Shep? You okay?" came up again unbidden through the glow of the Darvocets and that's when she realized this was Don, a faster form of Sheppard. *He's here to help*, she reminded herself, sure of things, moving toward the calmness in that voice. *He bought me lemonade.*

Rikki felt those eyes on her again, so she leaned her wrists on the table's edge. "I'm okay, really."

"Yeah, you said that a few times." Rikki heard Sheppard's tone again in Don's words. But that might have been all the Darvocets. She's got to be wrong about her ears. Except for those shoes he's the nicest guy she's ever hung with.

Two buses later, up in Hollywood, Rikki squatted up against a dumpster and Don stood. Rikki tossed the last of the pills down with her final sip of to-go lemonade, there in the alley. Off of Selma, she thinks, *Selma?* Maybe. Maybe Yucca. Who can tell? The arc of the finished pill bottle; tossed up and over her shoulder carelessly ended in the open dumpster. A look of surprise at that showed on her face.

"Good shot."

"Lucky," she apologized to his knees.

His shoes are so far from his nice voice. The thought struck her like a kick. But Rikki pushed it away in a long lasting breath, "I really hate things in my pockets."

"Why's that?"

"Dunno. Maybe it just reminds me I'm here."

"Ah." He stood, looking down at her. She felt it, in spite of the 14 Darvocets, or maybe because of them. "And that's too hard right?"

The back of her neck came un-numb for a second. She could sense him, his eyes maybe, making some decision. Rikki watched his shadow on the alley's gravel, shifting his shoulder like he was testing if it could heft something.

"Yep." Rikki set the empty lemonade cup down. A hand on the gravel trying to steady herself.

"I guess I'm like that too," he said. "I hate leaving a trace."

Rikki remembered her disappearing square of gauze on the bus. The empty wallets, vanishing in crevices no one would think to look in. Her head swam.

She didn't think first, and heard herself saying one more time, "I'm okay, really," just before she wasn't any longer.

Dead for a While

ON THE PLAYGROUND, we stood in line for the horizontal bars after lunch. Becca was behind me, because I may be small but I'm faster than most and I got there first. When you're in fourth you don't wanna be on the rings anymore; the boys can see your underwear. And they never let you forget it. But the horizontal bars area is at the end, near the third-grade rooms, and mostly you just have to give the littler kids a boost when it's their turn and they'll let you stay on as long as you like 'cause they know you're in Fourth.

It got to be my turn and I said, "Let's do Propellers."

And Becca said, "Ooo, yeah! But lemme be on top."

Propellers is for two. Both of you on the bars at the same time, one under and one on top. The top person sits on the bar with her hands a little farther out than usual, 'cause the bottom person puts her hands next to them, on the inside, and hooks her feet on the other's ankles. Then you drop your head back and let yourself lean waaay back and the gravity of the top spins you both backward around and around and around, like propellers.

Mostly, gravity keeps your dress down.

Becca liked being on top. She's taller, and if you're tall and take bottoms you can graze your head every time you go around. But I said, "No, I call tops, just duck your head this time," and she said, "Okay, Duff, but you owe me tops next time."

She weighs more than me, but I just liked tops more than bottoms, even though she pulls me down with her weight, and it's harder to get us started.

We must have spun for like fifteen minutes straight, the faces of the littler kids whipping past the back of my head like they were bats hanging upside down. We were bar hogs, staying on and spinning until the bell rang for Line Up.

"That was so much fun, my stomach hurts," I said, holding my side while we stood in Line Up to go back to class.

Becca leaned in over my left shoulder and whispered in my ear, "So much fun I went bald."

"So much fun I broke out in a rash," I whispered back, giggling. The stitch in my side grew sharper. "So much fun I wet myself."

"Quiet in Line Up!" The boy monitor for Sixths warned from up front.

"So much fun my leg fell off." She reached around to poke me in my side and I groaned, doubling over.

Becca and a girl monitor from the Fifths had walked me to

the nurse, and Becca told a lie to Miss Oliver, who showed up out of nowhere; that us being cousins, her mom should be called, 'cause she had a car. Becca knows my situation at home.

So, while I kept still on the cot and held the thermometer at the right angle, and felt how the nurse's cool hand relieved a bit of the pain, Becca apologized to her more than once for me throwing up so much and I listened to them whisper that my mom's work number wasn't any good any more, and that stomach flu was going around. Well, calling Becca's mom; that's what they finally did. Becca went back to class with Miss Oliver, and I got carried into the backseat of Mrs. Bettencourt's car.

Telephone poles and treetops and a cloudless sky rushed by the car's window, and though I tried my best not to moan, because of the rocking of the car, I failed. She glanced back at me then, but my eyes kept fading from seeing her face to where there was only white in front of me; maybe she turned front and kept driving, I don't remember, but I heard her say from far, far away, *Oh, my God.* Before I gave up, in my head, I added, *I am heartily sorry for having offended thee ...*

Someone shouted, "Okay, it's burst, let's get her in there," and the rolling cot I was on was rocking down a bright hall; the motion was pure murder. Then we were in a very cold room, and I heard, "So this is our barefoot countessa, hmm?", and a face came up over behind me, he smiled, and put a rubber smelling thing over my face, asking, "Can you count backwards from one hundred, Bright-Eyes?"

I nodded, but thought that I might never see Mama again in this life, so instead of counting, I breathed in and began, "Ah, *Mi Dios—*"

I can't remember if I made it to the part that goes: *I firmly resolve, with the help of Thy grace, to sin no more and to avoid the near occasions of sin.*

Mama had three things to say about me going to the hospital once they got me out of the surgery and she thought I was still under. Becca and my sister Barbie found Justine over at her friend Lydia's house, and Mrs. Bettencourt drove Justine, cause she's the oldest of us all, to Roy's to bring Mama back to the hospital. Mama must have been killer mad about disappointing the rest of Roy's time with her.

She must have wanted to say some things directly to my face because she hissed at me there on the bed as she walked in and my eyes were still closed; she knew I could hear her. She tossed her purse at my side and bumped the bed. Low, just for me, she told me: "Stop faking."

Mrs. Bettencourt and Justine were right behind her, so I didn't get slapped like I expected. I overheard the second thing, just when she turned and walked out; she asked Justine, "Who's gonna pay for this? Huh?"

The third thing she had to say was just to Mrs. Bettencourt. Well, anyone awake in the kid's ward may have heard it too; she and Mama were standing near my bed again. For parts of it, it was yelling done in whispers; "*Bullshit, Alice. I did come back; I'm here now, not like either of them,*" and: "*You don't have the slightest inkling what I've lost keeping this circus going.*"

I could even hear them off in the distance, after Mrs. Bettencourt said, "Later Reina, in the hall," and she'd tucked my covers tight and I could almost pretend I was back home, under the picture window in the front bedroom, extra blankets, donated from Chance's bed, up to my shivering chin. With the winter sunlight in through the curtains we'd made from sheets, glowing bright over my head. It was such a thing of beauty to see.

When I woke up I was on my back and my feet were freezing. It was the hospital still. The curtain thing around the bed was pulled nearly all the way closed; just a sliver of an opening at the foot of the bed. I wanted to curl up in a little ball, but I was too stiff. I wanted to pull the covers over my head, burrito-style, like I did at home, so I could go back to sleep. My stomach burned. When I pushed against the mattress with my feet, trying to turn on my side, I couldn't. Moving stung. Bad. I put my hand to where the stinging was and touched a bulky bandage, taped low, lower than my belly button, the size of a paperback book, but not so thick.

I let my eyes look sideways and around, trying my hardest to keep my hand pressed down and my body still. And that's when I felt Mama there, her head resting in her arms on the edge of my mattress. Like we do when we put our heads down on our desks at school for quiet time, or when we play Seven-Ups. No peeking.

She might be sleeping, I thought. So I stopped trying to move. But I felt so cold I started to shiver again and couldn't stop. The trembling made Mama twitch and she lifted her head with a jerk, pulling back until she was focused on where she'd woken up.

Our eyes met. "Hi, Mama," I said. "It's cold in here." She touched my forehead.

"I can ask them for another blanket."

"Where's my pajamas?"

"You don't need them."

"Okay."

We stayed there like that for a moment, in whispers. Mama, her eyes still all sleepy, and me, cold and stinging. She yawned. "They took your appendix out."

Propellers. So much fun my stomach hurts. "Oh." I was feeling sleepy again, myself. "Can I roll over?"

Mama stood and turned me on my side, gently, like I was an old lady, frozen and creaking, "There you go." She sat back down, propped on her elbows this time, chin in her hands. Her dark mascara was smudged, up under her eyes.

"You can put your head back down," I told her, and "I'm sorry," I added. She acted like she hadn't heard that; she stayed propped up. She yawned again. I wondered what would get her to listen. Then I said, "Can I go back to sleep?"

"Sure, Sugar. *Duerme ahorita.*" I looked at her longer, waiting. Maybe the slaps would be coming later. Then I pulled the sheet over my head. I kept my eyes open under there. My hands, in a prayer between my knees and my shoulders, cold and tight. Waiting. Finally I felt her lower her head down to the bed.

From under there, I whispered, "Mama? I'm really sorry."

Outside of the curtain there were shifting noises and

little coughs. I heard footsteps moving past us. But they stopped short and stepped back to my bed. I held my breath. They were probably looking in at Mama sleeping; maybe she shouldn't be here in the night.

"*Ay, no,*" a lady's voice whispered from the foot of the bed, "*Raúl, mira, la niña está muerta.*"

There was a squeak of the curtain and then Raúl's whispering, "*Pobrecita … qué lastima,*" before they tiptoed away from us. I waited a second more before I peeked out from under my sheet—Mama's eyes were open, inches from mine. She was smiling. She lifted an eyebrow, and mouthed, "*qué lastima,*" such a shame, and I smiled too at the story they saw; me, dead still, under the sheet and Mama's head bowed on the bed. Then I closed my eyes and fell back asleep. The next time I woke up there was another blanket on me, but Mama was gone. I lay there wondering if I'd dreamed my playing dead for a while and her tired smile.

"Her drain's not as productive as I'd expect it to be," the Doctor was telling the other doctors who were standing around my bed looking in at my uncovered stitches. There was a little amber tube sticking out of the side of my stitches, near my bellybutton, like a miniature butterscotch lawn hose. And greenish-yellowish stuff was leaking out of it, no matter how often the doctor peeked at it. She flipped through the pages she held and said, "Looking at the serum iron level, and iron binding I'd add anemia, considering her actual age and this low weight. These people." She sighed, "We'll keep her a bit longer, till she's in better shape for discharge."

I looked down at my bare middle and exposed hip bones and tried to be funny. "Maybe if you stood me on my head and leaned me up against a wall I'd drain better." But no one except the nurse bothered to smile.

Every day I got helped out of bed and I'd walk, careful and bent a little, out to the nurse's counter. I'd look down the hall to the left and the right, but no Mama. One day a lady with a cart of books gave me one about Origami; there wasn't any folding paper but it was nice looking at the steps anyway. It wasn't Mama, but it was just the same, the book lady was being nice. My smiling nurse noticed my origami book when she brought me lunch one day, and I showed her the peacocks and the giraffes and the lion you could fold to show his fangs in his open mouth. The next time she saw me she handed me a thin telephone book, saying, "Knock yourself out, kiddo," before she checked my nonproductive drain again.

I folded every animal in the big book, careful not to pull the needle from the back of my hand. And gave the animals around to the other kids. Some of the parents who came visiting looked in my book and asked me for alligators and dragons 'cause they'd seen me doing the harder ones. So I was very popular when they came to take their kids home; the parents all hugged me good-bye, wiggling their animals *so long* at me, and some kissed my forehead.

With the bunnies, I folded them in Big, Medium, Small, and Smallest size. And my nurse took them to her counter and they stayed there, day after day, looking cozy sitting, all together, like a regular bunny family. I touched the smallest one every time I stood there, waiting in the hall.

Then one day our worker, Mr. St. John, walked into my ward holding a yellow balloon that bobbed on a fancy curling ribbon. He looked smart and tall and clean, and, well, white. He searched all around then he saw me in my bed. "There she is," he said, as he handed me the balloon. "Are you ready to get out of here?"

I hadn't seen anyone I knew since that night with Mama, maybe eleven days ago. Someone did know I was still alive. I looked up at the yellow balloon and like a little crybaby, I broke into tears.

In the car he found out about Mama, her not visiting after the first night. But he promised not to say anything to her when I asked him not to. I hate lying, but sometimes you have to ask folks to do it anyway.

So to make the time pass I started up an old game we used to play on Hockert Street—when he was just getting to know our family. We talked about the Best Life. The life I'd lead once we grew up and got out on our own. The life he was probably living right now.

Mr. St. John, he got it wrong again, and was saying stuff about ponies; how many he was gonna have and where he'd shop for them, where he'd be keeping them and all. So to help his story, since he'd promised about Mama, I acted like the pony-order guy, and asked, "And how will you have your pony served, Mr. St. John?"

"Why, with blue chaps and a blue vest of course," he said. "Trimmed with silver tassels, please, and umm … A black and silver hat on the side, I think." We laughed.

"And you, Miss Chavez," he asked. "How would you like your pony?"

And I thought a moment, because ponies weren't really on my Best Life list, but I didn't want him to stop and not play anymore.

"Please bring my usual pony with blue and yellow and pink ribbons braided in her mane and tail," I answered. "Yes, a little light brown one I think, and make sure my pony only allows barefoot girls to ride. No shoes, spurs, or boys, please."

Then he pulled to stop at my house and we saw her coming down the block from the bus and Mr. St. John said, "Shit, your Mom," and I couldn't stop myself; I looked all around for a way to run before I remembered who I was with.

"She took a short day. I told her I'd be bringing you home."

And I realized. *Oh, Man. A short day from work and just because of me.* She was gonna kill me for sure. We both stepped out of the car and waited for what would be coming.

The pain arrows in my side from my new scar made it hard to worry and be strong at the same time. But standing there I felt lighter, like I could fly now, after the operation. "You don't have to lie after all, Mr. St. John," I said. "I'm not gonna."

Once Mr. St. John left it was just Barbie and me in the kitchen, talking to Mama. I slipped into a kitchen chair and just tried to catch my breath, my side was killing me.

"A half day off for this." Mama turned to me.

"You didn't have to, I would've told him not to call." I said, not looking at Barbie.

"The truth, Duff. What have I told you about that?"

"Don't do it without permission first," I recited.

"Don't you get smart with me, Duffy." She slapped at the table top and made me jump. "You think you can make me look bad? Get on his good side and make me look like shit? Well you can just go to your room and figure out how you're gonna get dinner tonight cause you're not getting any from my table, Miss-I'm-so-smart."

"But Mama—I—"

"No buts—get out of my face. Now." So I went. And didn't eat dinner, which added to the feeling of being so much lighter now. But at least I didn't lie. And learning not to lie was something that *was* on my Best Life list. Even it if meant giving up a chance at good times with Mama, all sleepy and nice in the dark, her forgetting for some reason and not slapping me. The Best Life meant never being dead for awhile, that was the other thing I added to the list.

Behind the Wheel of Something

CHRISTINA WAITS IN front of her fourth motel office, lacing her numb fingers around a cup of courtesy coffee, and refuses to stare at the height of the Rockies looming up in her left periphery. Sober as a judge, all she can think of is five days previous and her step-dad Harrison waiting outside her work. Sitting behind the wheel of his truck, just slightly buzzed, the sweet smell of reefer in the truck cab.

Christina finds herself to be a bit of a lead foot on this trip, pushing the van on relentlessly. But Harrison maneuvered the roads home that Wednesday with the utmost care on the slick streets. The oncoming lights on the wet pavement skewed the divider lines and the truck jerked when Harrison tapped his breaks more than he really needed to, nervous; avoiding all the ghosts the rain brought on. He pulled into their driveway and set the parking break, removed the key from the ignition, then just sat.

She knew she'd be going right then.

Knew it like she knew their breath fogging the windshield. She saw Nicky's nose peeking from behind the blinds, saw his fat furry paw in the picture window. White. For some reason she thought, *I'll have to vacuum the drapes.* Now in the biting morning cold she hasn't a clue where that came from. Harrison's voice nags at her from two and a half states away.

"Got some questions, slugger. You up for that?"

Seven. All over again. Christina's twisting her foot, just like then. "Okay."

"You're not working at the paper anymore?"

"No."

"I picked you up from work at a place you don't work at anymore? Any reason to talk about that?"

"None."

Now she looks at her new—used—van parked in number 233 and remembers the sun that afternoon, low enough to skirt under the rainclouds and cut a swatch of fading light on the driveway next to them, between the two houses. How it didn't touch the truck. Dimness there.

Dimness like the kitchen that morning, when it all became clear to her. She'd won.

From that day on Christina bowed and strained under a numbered list of wishes and a list of disappointments that she'd written up a week earlier. Bowed under the too-loud ticking of the kitchen clock, Harrison sat at the table drinking his morning pot of coffee, his empty bong at his elbow and the usual murk of sticky smoke wreathing his head and shoulders.

From as far back as Christina could remember, way back when she was small, even when her mother was still there with them, Harrison's morning ritual started this way. Three bowls in the bong and a full pot of coffee just for him. That was breakfast.

He blamed it on being a lineman for the phone company: *Up this pole in the wind and rain, down that smelly vault all fuckin' summer, all kinds of crumby weather, hell of a life for a poet.*

Day seven finds her two hundred and fifty three miles farther north, and angry that the night auditor of Motel 8 won't make eye contact even though it's just the two of them, here at a quarter to seven in the morning, waiting out the hiss of the brown-scorched coffee pot he's set up next to a cold silver waffle maker. The silence got to her worse than she expected it would. She could've stayed home to get silence like this.

Here she was on her own, and the world was proving to be no more than a mirror of her own depressing kitchen. She cheered herself up by slipping her hand into her pocket and touching the newly revised wish list she'd folded up there, before bringing her bag down from the room. That, and the folded scrap of orange kept her going, mile after mile.

At home, the years had passed. Her mother had kicked it in a pretty ugly way. The trees out front and Christina herself grew taller; both of them growing up past Harrison's 5"6', but Harrison's song remained the same.

One Tuesday, about five weeks prior to vacuuming the drapes, she'd asked him, "Hey, gimme a number," pulling a chocolate-chip muffin and a can of cat food from the fridge.

"God, it's Wednesday tomorrow, isn't it?" But he didn't have any numbers for her, "Nope. Nothin' here for you sweetie."

Christina fed Nicky, touched the top of his head, and reached for her house key and bus pass from the bowl on the counter near the telephone. "I'll leave your dinner in the fridge," she told Harrison, like every other morning.

On day eight of her trip she wonders if she should place a call to let him know she's okay. Already that house seems so very far away. Another life where she lived on Heil Avenue, in El Centro, California; one of the newest and poorest of all of California's fifty-eight counties. It bordered both Arizona and Mexico. A county shaped like the zipper tongue on an open jacket. *Birthplace of Cher*, Christina thinks whenever she sees a state map.

She skips the next opportunity to stop and drives twelve hours right on through, leaving day nine behind her like the pair of white socks she's forgotten she hung up in the bathroom at the last Holiday Inn. Memories of the dark house keep her foot to the pedal.

Before the trees had gotten big enough to shade the kitchen window, and because of its southern exposure, her mom took to calling it *Hell Avenue*. That was back when they first moved in, the family only arriving seven months before that day in January: *rain, red-light runner.*

The van makes a shuddering sound on inclines after another eight hours on the road and she can all but hear Harrison saying '*Stop, dimwit. What are you trying to do to me?*' And Christina chases that tone of voice away by dreaming up her mother singing to her that last Christmas. A song she made up about Hell Avenue and only minding it in the winters. '*La, dee, dum, and the summers, dee, dee, dah.* Sing with me baby.'

But it's the beginning of February now. So, after forcing herself to take one more stop and placing a wake-up call for 3:00a.m., she's more pissed at Harrison than ever before. Mostly about the number of years she didn't drive. Didn't want to see Harrison's stricken face if she ever climbed behind the wheel of something.

She's thinking about Harrison's bong as that song comes on the radio, some dead singer crooning about a perfect love. Thinking of the occasional speedball he does when his pal Danny comes by, smelling like the bakery; all yeasty and sweet. She laughs to herself, these lyrics; love songs running under the tough talk every time those two get together. Harrison thinking she doesn't know about the drugs; about how after all these years he still sits alone in the garage when he needs a good cry; about her being the witness to all that, all these years. No. She's not gonna stop and call. Not gonna tell anyone. Not even Harrison.

So now, here she is, nearly at the Canadian Border, Winnipeg just a dog-leg to her right. Nightfall coming. Another stop in an anonymous room and more time to ponder what's coming.

Her. Sitting on some slippery quilted bedspread; the TV going just for the noise. Her feet gone numb, maybe from all the steering and driving. Maybe not though. Questions running like gerbils on a wheel. With this orange lotto ticket, and her hands shaking, there'll be a hollow feeling behind her forehead, and she'll ask herself for the tenth time: *Shit. What now?* But there's no sense waiting for an answer, even if it was only going to be, "Nope. Nothin' here for you, sweetie."

Straight and Solid

WHAT I REMEMBER most from that day was his nails. Thin bands of bone white, curt in length, clipped like the words he had for my mother. He found me in Granny's sewing room, now made up into a bedroom for me. Me sitting on the floor looking at the photograph my mother had slipped into the last book she knew I was reading. A picture of my brother, Danny Ray, looking down at me, and me, nine years old, frowning into the camera.

"What'cha doing on the floor?" Uncle Joshua snatched the picture from my hand before I realized he was in the room. I jumped up, pulling at each leg of my shorts.

"Didn't want to mess up the spread."

He nodded, flicked the picture to his chest. "C'mon." He walked down the hall.

I followed into the dark of the kitchen. He sat. I stood. Joshua looked over his shoulder toward the back of the house, then tapped my picture where he had set it between us on the table.

"Child, you're old enough to know the truth. Your mama's good as gone now. Best you get that into your mind, straight an' solid."

He said a few other things too, but mostly I remember that. And the sound of his nails in the dimness. His finger so squared and wide it covered my face each time it came down over the 'me' in the photo.

He said, "Me, I always thought your Ma was a fine, pretty girl, even in them damn dungarees she wore. Spirited. Alice tried hard to liven up her world. Like the zig-zags on this picture, cut 'em with sewing clippers—" He looked up at me.

I nodded, "—pinking shears."

"Yeah, that's right." He ran his thumbnail down the picture's edge. *Dit-dit-dit-dit-dit.* "Pinking... Now, your Granny's" *dit-dit-dit,* "she knew her for a whore. From as far back as you are here in this." *Tap-tap,* my face disappearing again. "Never in a dress, hanging with all color of boys, then with them unnatural women, might as well a'been boys they-selves. It never mattered to Alice."

I looked down to the grayed linoleum. His voice kept on, even lower than before, "Your brother—black blood in that kid. Can't see it in his hair or nothing, but it's there all the same. That's why she didn't send him on with you. It just wouldn'ta been right. We're Christian. Like to like, your Granny says."

Tap-tap-tap.

"And now with that sickness that's got your ma—" he stared right into my eyes, "your Granny won't allow her name in this house, so don't you even try."

He waited for me, watched for tears or fear, maybe both. But I only looked to the picture, looked to Danny's eyes, and to my frown, like Joshua had said, straight an' solid. I guess it was then I promised myself these people would never matter to me either.

"Anyway—" he reached for my picture, ripping it in half, crumbling my brother in his solid fist, leaving me torn, alone on the table, "—thank Jesus, you're with us now."

Exercise

"**O**H, GOD!" LINDSAY sighed.

Mimi was biting her earlobe. Her fingertips played rough with Lindsay's nipples as Mimi's mouth worked its way down her neck, canines grazing her jugular.

"Oh, Gawd…"

"Quiet," Mimi told her, her mouth full of clavicle now.

"Quiet?"

Mimi touched a fingertip to Lindsay's lips, whispered, "You don't get to talk."

Lindsay ground her hips against Mimi's, "But, I wanna—"

"—No."

"Why—ahhhh—not?" Mimi's mouth started down Lindsay's stomach, licked at her navel, kept going.

"You've been bad," Mimi said, down to business. Her hands held Lindsay's hips still. Tongue darting.

Then Lindsay's started singing, in a high kiddie voice,

"Hap-pee-Birth-day-to-me… Hap-pee-Birth-day-to—" That's when Mimi shifted right and bit her inner thigh. Hard.

The radio alarm went off and Mimi found herself on her stomach, surrounded by too many pillows, cats. Just her. Alone again. For the fifth month now. Her legs tangled in the sheets, the quilt slipped half off the bed because there was no one next to her to need it.

She propped herself up on both elbows, pushed her index fingers into the corners of her eyes, then she wiggled deeper under the bedding. Kids were singing. On the radio. That's where the birthday song came from.

She slapped at the off button, crawled out of the bedding tangle and squinted. 4:50a.m. She squinted again but couldn't make out where her glasses might be. There wasn't any sunlight yet.

She thought again about selling everything, driving Northeast until she reached Canada. Mimi's latest fantasy. Divestiture.

But she knew, even if she did all that, the dreams wouldn't stop. She stood up, went to feed the cats.

At the start of her 5:30a.m. spin class the instructor had taken a poll. They decided that whilst they were all seriously committed to the ungodly starting time, there was no good reason for the lights to be up all the way, so they rode their stationary bikes in dimness. They faced East while Ann, the instructor, motivated them by saying cheery things like, "OKAY, guys! Let's ride hard and see who throws up first."

The song *Walking on Broken Glass* began playing out of

Ann's boom box and Mimi cranked up the resistance on her bike, lowered her head and pushed it harder than usual, which was pretty dammed hard. She rode like that till her thighs burned as much as the tears running down her face did.

Later that day, after work, Mimi drove with her right hand crossed over at eleven o'clock on the wheel, her left elbow up on the door, the hand cradling her neck as if without the support her head would topple off. On the radio Huey Lewis was really getting on her nerves.

Squinting into the sunset, occasionally steering with her knees, she concentrated on punching at the other five radio presets, and tried her best to remember to breathe.

In through the nose. Out through the mouth. Work that diaphragm, she heard Eddie, her shrink, say. *Fill the stomach on the inhales. Push it all out by caving in the stomach on the exhale.*

Six stations and all of them pissed her off.

Still one-handed, she glided left and right through traffic like her car was a joystick and the five clotted lanes ahead a game of Tetris.

Eddie. What a stupid name for a shrink. She inhaled. A raised F-250 took a slot ahead of her. The truck wore a bumper sticker: fancy red letters on a black background. She squinted. Once she figured out the font and then its short message: *Fuck Off.* All she could say to the windshield, after a pretty good exhale, was, "Get in line, dude."

Maybe, she thought, *I shouldn't go to the bar. I've got workout stuff with me; maybe I should go to the gym instead.*

Her neck still cupped in her hand, her vision just skewed enough at this angle to make the mopey 5p.m. drive interesting.

A couple of Seven and Sevens? Or an hour of laps then some weight work? She asked herself this a lot, even now; going on three years sobriety. Even now she still had to ask.

Eddie's voice again: *Getting drunk, wired, or working out, alcohol, speed or endorphins—either way, Mimi, you're still spending your time getting altered—the choice is yours on which method you want to go for. Since it looks like avoidance is something you seem to be stuck with.*

Stupid-ass name, Eddie.

She hadn't told him yet, about how the dreams wouldn't stop. Or about how she'd turned the ringer off on her phone at home because she couldn't stand the sound of it not ringing. Or about the greeting card she'd sent, back in April. The words painstakingly spelled out with little scrap-booking stickers that looked like Scrabble tiles. The outside reading: *I missed your b'day? Oh, Hon, I'm sorry...* on the inside, more tile stickers: *Wanna Fuck?*

He waved a novel at her during one session; the dust jacket's title had the words *Electric* and *God* in it. That alone got on her nerves but he'd read her face and said, "Hold your horses there." He leaned in to read to her from a hot pink sticky he'd plucked from its pages: *'It's not hard to fall in love. The hard part is to love somebody who might actually do you some good.'* Then he handed her a bigger blue sticky, to keep.

Careful, bold block letters. It read: *Is it good for Mimi?*

Man, her neck hurt.

She thought about Lindsay. Then worked at not doing that. A lot of geese were up in the sky over the freeway. They flew in groups, silhouetted up against the few clouds that grew pinker and pinker by the minute.

She slipped into auto-pilot, watching the geese, some in V-formations, some in long straight lines, and some in broken formation with one V's legs shorter than the other.

One lone goose flew too far ahead of one group to be part of their pattern. But it wasn't fast enough to be part of the next V it followed.

That's me, she thought.

Then, out loud she asked the radio, "Who sings this?"

She thought of Lindsay's hand that one time, in its own V of sorts, two finger here, two fingers there, and her thumb moving all on its own, maddeningly slow and random, till Mimi nearly bit into the pillows stacked under her.

"Who the hell sings this?"

She decided, glanced in her rear-view mirror and slid into the exit lane. The Bar.

I'll only order Diet Cokes, she promised herself.

"Who the hell sings this?"

She inhaled. Bar or gym, she'd be alone while surrounded. And that was better than being at home. Alone. One had Buffalo Wings, one had a hot tub.

Let it all out on the exhale, she reminded herself.

It seemed to Mimi that, since Lindsay and that loss, her days were measured out in minutes and miles.

It had been even worse at the beginning; then her queen

bed had stuff strewn everywhere, toppling with whatever she touched, day after day. It all ended up on her bed; library books, papers from work, CDs, clothes. And a small Mimi space carved in the middle.

Once, she'd told Eddie: *I didn't have my glasses on and I reached over to pet the cat but it was just a dark fleecy pullover bunched under my hand.*

Back then, she'd come home, slide right under the covers first thing; she was that exhausted. Then, after she'd wake up four hours later, sweaty and tangled, she'd pull off the stuff she wore without even getting out from under the quilt.

Underwear, socks, bras, shirts, tank tops; discarded clothes migrated from under her blankets to end up piled along with the overflow of unopened mail along the side of her bed, making new, difficult daily obstacle courses for the cats.

Then she remembered exercise. And that helped. A lot. Four months ago she'd broken down and started seeing Eddie, on Wednesdays. "I'm psychic at times," she'd told him at their first meeting, "but dumb too; keep walking right into the danger. I never take what I see seriously, and I want to stop that now. I'm ready, I think…" And now everything was a little better. Her room was a bit neater, at least.

Calmer. Measured. Minutes, miles.

The weight fell off. The silhouette of Mimi's abs became a bit more defined. Her calf muscles lost their little layer of fat. When she flexed her arm you could actually see the muscles move. She was able to run part of the three miles she walked most days at seven each evening.

Sure she was still lonely, but at least these small parts of her day weren't spent burrowed under quilts, unconscious. The cats were happier with the easier access to the foot of her bed.

But the dream still kept coming. And while she was awake that echo of *Wait. Please. Just wait a second* and the click of Lindsay hanging up. Saturdays were best. If anything could be called that.

She made up lists and stuck to them, for the most part.

Her Wednesdays—there she made the effort, tried her hardest, almost let herself tell Eddie, "It's like she had—"

In some sessions she found it possible, even easy; to let just one crying breath out, then hold the rest in. *Ready* was a relative term some weeks.

In her dream it was the first time they met for dinner. They laughed easily. It was a good time. In her mind she thought: Finally, thank the gods for a friend. *Out in the parking lot Mimi smiled over her car roof, and in the dimness she was sure Lindsay was smiling too before she ducked into her own car. Mimi stood, watched till the interior light went out. Lindsay drove away. In the dream neither of them noticed the man waiting in the shadow of the trees.* Most times Mimi didn't wake in time, trapped in it until the screams opened her eyes. Eddie only asked the one time what she thought the connection might be. "—I don't know…" She ended up saying, though she did.

Mimi was at a brunch with a few friends. Their patio table was full of waffles, mimosas, plain OJ for Mimi. Jenna coughed into her napkin, whispered, "Oh shit."

"What, hon?" Maureen asked, frowning toward Jenna's plate.

"Lindsay."

No one turned to look. All four looked at Mimi. Then she felt the hand on her shoulder, "Hey Mims." Suddenly the table unfroze; more coughing, shifting of silverware, outright glares. "Hi, everybody." No one answered. Mimi inhaled, waited for the hand to go away. Instead, Lindsay squeezed; "You're getting thinner."

Mimi leaned in to the table, reached for the orange juice, pulled away from Lindsay's touch. "Umm-hum." She felt like she'd made a wimpy move, felt stupid for not speaking up.

"Well, it looks good on you," Lindsay tried again, "Suits you."

Mimi was uncomfortable doing this in front of the two couples. Out in the open. She glanced at her watch, tilted her head back, looked into Lindsay's eyes, and in a low voice asked; "It's been a whole two minutes, shouldn't you be running away from me by now?"

Lindsay stopped. Dropped her hand to her side then turned, walked toward the ladies room. Long fast strides. The others murmured around the table.

"Shit." Mimi sighed, tossed her napkin on the tablecloth, "I'll be back."

"Want me to come?" Maureen asked.

Mimi shook her head. "I know the drill."

She hurried, caught the rest room door just before it closed behind Lindsay. She slipped in. Locked it behind them.

"I'm sorry. Me and my mouth."

Lindsay leaned against the sink, arms crossed, "No. I don't think you're a bit sorry."

Mimi extended a hand, "Truce?" She watched Lindsay consider the hand, grimacing. As one, they both walked into a hug. Then Lindsay turned Mimi around, unzipped her jeans, slipped her hand in and bit Mimi's neck, "I hate you right now."

"I know," Mimi arched her back, moaned, "I know."

"No, not hate, really." Her breath in Mimi's ear, "I'm just—empty inside. A part of me—ahhh—loves you."

"I don't want you to love me, baby." Mimi leaned into her, gritted her teeth.

"But, I do. I do love you."

Mimi thought: *Such bullshit.* She let loose a ragged breath, like a tea kettle, fixing to scream. "No. You don't."

"I do."

"No. No, you don't."

They watched each other's faces in the wide mirror, still panting.

Lindsay smiled, sad, touched Mimi's heart with a fingertip, spoke to their reflection, low, a secret, "Just cause I can't," she reached to turn on the tap, rinsed her hand, "doesn't mean I don't." She moved to unlock the door and like that, once again, she walked out.

Mimi studied her face in the mirror. She remembered her dream, after their first time together: *Lindsay walking into Mimi's bedroom, sitting on her bed, grabbing at her throat and squeezing. Mimi, reaching out her hands, trying only to say PLEASE.* After she'd woke up screaming she shook her head and thought; *That'll never happen.*

It took another three weeks for Mimi to mention her rape dreams to Eddie. Another few sessions to allow they were actually memories mixed up in dreams of Lindsay. It made the issue of Lindsay's departure sound like Saturday cartoons. Now, days since, Eddie was getting tired of Mimi's avoidance. Mimi refused to revisit it, instead she asked him the riddle about what do you get crossing an onion with a donkey.

Eddie lowered his chin, listened, tapped his knee then sighed, "That may be the most expensive punch line you tell all month." So Mimi finally allowed them to get back into the dreams. Then sneaky Eddie steered her into that last phone call, where Lindsay had hung up without hearing Mimi out. And somehow that led them into trauma.

"Here's how trauma normally operates in babies," Eddie said, leaning in for it. "We're all made up of parts, right? Heart, lungs, muscles, nerves, chemicals and stuff. We're wired to react to fear, to stimulation. You pick up a baby and hold her up in the air and her body responds: adrenaline. Her feet aren't on the ground, what's going on? Maybe it'll be bad.

"Maybe good. Maybe someone who loves her wants to give a tickle. Maybe not. Either way, you put her back down and things go back to normal, right? The chemicals recede. She's breathing normal again. Sits up or rolls over. Closes her eyes. Smiles. No problem.

"But some babies have it hard, it's never safe. It's always adrenaline for bad reasons, they get stuck. The chemicals don't lower back into a normal range. They're never sure: Is this a whirl in his arms or will I be bashed into the wall? These babies are re-wired because of all the abuse. So days later every noise like the vacuum is a signal to freeze. Maybe every time she leaves the crib her back tenses up. Every smell of garlic means someone's gonna scream and bleed. Her reaction to other people becomes: Don't come near me, I'll get hurt."

Mimi tried hearing it, but it was all too real. She'd have to work at getting there. She'd have to exercise first. She was ready for heartache, but not this. Drinks were coming if she ever got onto that topic.

Mimi could hear the phone ringing as she opened the garage door and stepped into the hall. Two, three rings. She was unsteady on her feet. How was it that she had no problem driving all fucked up, but walking was such a chore? She bounced off the walls in the hall as she bent to scratch the cat's head. Nearly falling forward, "Who's mummy's good pussycat?" She wanted to know, needed an answer, "Who's mummy's furry baby, huh?"

She heard her own words to Eddie in the session: "*He reached for my throat, pushing me down. 'Wait', I tried saying, 'Please. Just wait a second'. But he wouldn't let me talk. I was sure if I could just talk he wouldn't be doing this.*

He might've been squeezing till I stopped making noise, but

I don't know for sure. Everything went black."

Mimi had looked up at Eddie. There were tears in his eyes. *"Like Lindsay... why couldn't they let me talk?"* She wanted to know.

Eddie told her, "Take a breath, hon."

Five rings, six, seven. More bouncing as she made her way to the bedroom. Her shoulder was gonna hurt if she kept this up. Eight rings. Nine. She reached the phone and picked it up, glancing at the clock, a quarter to two.

She knew it was Lindsay. She was psychic, but dumb about it.

"Aunt Sally's home for wayward girls, Spike speaking." Mimi listened. Then exhaled. Set her gym bag down, "Hi, baby."

Her feet left the floor, her back tensed up. She thought: Maybe it'll be bad.

She breathed. Maybe good.

Songs for a Lion

FIRST THING IN the morning they'll be coming for Suzette and Daniel. My babies. That worker, she'll come up these dark stairs. Without a glance at me she'll take my kids down to her car. She'll drive them to foster homes, away from here. I know I should've been stronger while I had a chance. I should've held on longer. I can dream they'll be set down in a lighter place, maybe a better place. But either way it's a done deal.

I should've just filled out their forms without trembling. That's what gave me away to the woman. They caught me unprepared. Just pieces of paper—paper, not snakes. No reason to tremble. But I was so tired. Still, why did I cry? Now this worker, she sees I can't cope. They've been around, talked with the neighbors; no way to keep my babies now.

It's a shame, since Suzette's just memorized our phone number. Four years old, and she's got it down. Daniel sounded so proud, making the grand introduction from the kitchen doorway. Stepping aside so cute, to present Suzette wearing her good church shoes; that little blue sun suit with the ducks.

"Three-three-seven-two-seven-oh-one," she recited, looking up and away for the numbers. I tried so hard to keep from grinning, seeing Danny there to the side, mouthing the numbers like a ventriloquist and Suzette a life-sized doll. Suzette's blue sun suit, white string straps tied at the back of her neck; the straps tangled in her curly black hair when she bowed from the waist, so deep and serious. *Jet black hair,* I taught her to say. She bowed. Her head nearly touched the toes of those shiny shoes. She loved any chance to get those shoes on her feet. *Princess shoes,* she called them. Daniel was so proud of his baby sister.

The two of them'll be okay as long as they're together. I can say it, and I do. But believing is something else.

So now what I've got is to say goodbye; a small time to give them a world full of mama comforts before tomorrow comes. My head feels so heavy; the clock over the stove says 4:30. When did so many hours slip away?

They're fussing at each other. Daniel tries to keep Suzette from opening the refrigerator again. She says she dreamed at nap time. "The refrigalator, it was full—bacon, real peaches, saggetti and orange cheese."

I know about the empty spaces on the shelves. The worker's been over it with me: "Staples," she called them. "Your house always needs the staples, at the least." I remember my mother's kitchen pantry; rows and rows of cans in neat order. She loved stacking in the five pound sacks of rice, flour, beans and sugar—I wanted to tell the worker about that—how I knew, about the '*at the least*' stuff. Really, I did.

I tell Daniel. "Go on. Let her. She can't believe what you say if she can't see it's true." So Daniel drops his hand. And Suzette's shoulders sag when she sees it's still true. She sighs. "Still empty."

I scoop her up into my arms, spin her around the cold kitchen till she giggles. I whisper, "Honey, one day you'll live in a house with food in the icebox, the cupboards, the hall closet, under your bed—there'll be so much food you'll have to give some to Puppet and Lisa down the hall."

She weighs nothing in my arms.

As I spin her she shrieks, "Danny! There's two refrigalators. No. No. There's *three* refrigalators. Mama's gonna get food for all of them." I snuggle her neck below her tiny ear, and breathe her giggles into my memory. "Love you, baby." Danny spins along next to me, so the two of them will be the same kind of dizzy when they fall to the floor.

He's so small for nine. The worker, she looked at him twice when I said, "Nine, he's nine." I used to wonder why he always tried to do and feel what Suzette did. Jealousy? I thought maybe it was. Until I found Danny squinting, trying to describe what was going on with the ambulance outside. "It's so I can protect her, Mom," he told me. "I copy what she sees to check what might be scary or make her cry." He called the truck 'the big red thing under the lights'. That was before I found out. Suzette's eyes. Then we had to go to the Clinic to get her glasses. Maybe he stays small to keep her company.

I give Daniel a hug too. Then I step over them on the floor to reach for my backpack. Maybe I missed a cigarette down at the bottom. A lotto ticket. Or a cure for this pressure I can't keep from pounding in me, calling me away. Maybe I'll find—anything.

Maybe.

"Turn on the radio, baby. Let's have some tunes."

Daniel twists the volume knob, up to the red nail polish mark.

"Mama," Suzette asks, "since you're home can we turn it higher?" The mark is so that they'll have music while I'm at work but not so loud anyone guesses they're home without me. I think about the warehouse jobs I couldn't hang on to these last months, all the jobs I tried to try for, if only I kept from trembling. I think about the way my voices warn I'll hurt my own babies. I think, *these are my kids, this is our last night,* my *last chance.*

I say "Go on—crank it, sweetie."

A song I sang to Daniel when he was still a baby comes on. Those lyrics, like my mom's voice scolding me. It's my fortune coming true, when all it used to be was this tune, a simple song in my ear. Where was it along the way the meaning changed to my life?

I don't find any overlooked cigarettes or lotto tickets. Instead, I let out a squeak, my eyes wide. The kids' eyes are even larger when they see the three stunted crayons I pull from the backpack. Blue, purple, green.

Suzette has chewed up most of the crayons that came in the last Christmas bag from the church, a deed she's heartily sorry for. But still I had to give her a punishment for doing it. When I finally let her up from the bed after a full twenty minutes of penance on the evils of eating crayons, she pleaded her case, "But Mama, I only ate the ice cream colors." I hand these crayons to Daniel for safety.

He runs to the living room to find newspaper for coloring on, Suzette at his heels. I can hear the loveseat scraping across the floorboards as they bounce from it into the bedroom. I smile in the empty kitchen, calling out, "I don't care how excited you are. Put my bed back where you found it!" I smile at being able to tease about their reasons for running. Maybe kid-sized miracles are all that's left to discover.

They can't find any newspaper, so Daniel asks to go down to the curb to look in the can for some. The trash is right near the bus bench; riders sometimes toss their papers just before they board.

"OK, but don't go looking in any other can. Just the one by the bench. Hear? Just that one, Danny."

Suzette is struggling to get her princess shoes on. I say, "Nah-uh, baby, you stay in."

"But, Mama—"

"Honey, let him do it." How do I explain broken glass, what it costs at the emergency room, when all she sees is a chance to run up and down the stairs with her brother? "No, Suz."

"Dannnny," Suzette begs.

Daniel looks from me to her and negotiates: "Can she wait at the top of the stairs?"

"Can she promise not to step off of them?" I ask.

"Oh, yes," she promises.

"Go." They tear to the door. "Leave the door open so I can hear you." In the still of the kitchen I turn the backpack upside down onto the table, hoping something will shake loose. I sing along to the radio.

Then I hear Suzette's voice, high. Yelling from the street.

I get out into the hall in a second. Daniel's run halfway up the stairs, Suzette in his arms. Her legs are kicking. His arms are around her middle. His eyes over her head are wide, bright. I yell. "What? What happened? What?"

At the top of the stairs I grab her from him. Hold her out in front of me, inspecting from all angles. Where's the blood? "Danny!" she screams, arching in my hands, "Danny," pointing, "from the trash." I turn to check him for a sign of what's gone wrong. He's holding something out to me. He spreads it to show me, front and back. A crumpled five-dollar bill. It's real. "From the trash!" Suzie repeats.

I stare a moment, then sit down hard, right there in the doorway. Five dollars. From the trash. When I look up Danny is watching, but Suzette has found a knee scab to peel as she hops on one foot. Only Danny's eyes can see my tears come. I nod, "Milk. Danny, get your shoes on this time. Yeah, baby," I add before Suzette can begin to beg, "you go, too."

This time I stand and watch from the window until they disappear into the corner market.

I hum with the radio, open the cupboard door. Shit. There are no staples here. This place has a small bag of pearl barley; Bisquik, but the box is so light when I shake it; a cup of confectioner's sugar in a twisted blue plastic bag; three fingers of cooking oil; a nearly empty jar of strawberry jam.

The worker's voice sounds in my ears: *This won't do, Reina.* But it has to. What else is there? I hear Danny's key in the lock and decide. I pull down the ingredients I'll use for their final dinner with me.

"Mama, Mrs. Rice says to tell you this—" Suzette hangs onto the sink counter as she gets set to deliver the message. But something takes her attention. She swings her foot out behind her till the sole of her shiny shoe nearly touches the back of her head. "Hey, Mama? What do sea monsters eat when they're in lingland?"

"England, Suz, not lingland," Danny says.

"Yeah, Mama, Englan. What do they eat?"

"Sea monsters?" Suzie swings her leg back again, waiting. "Uh, English toffee?" I say. She looks to the second judge, Danny shakes his head no.

"Guess again, Mama." The jitters in her legs demand an answer.

"I give up, Suz, what?"

"Fish and Ships!" she yells, falling to the floor laughing. Danny grins from the table. "Fish and Ships!" Suzie shrieks again, "Get it, Mama?"

"That's great, Roo. Fish and Ships."

"Danny, get the poem book; let's hear some while I do dinner."

"Me!" Suzette yells. "I'll get it," scrabbling up from the floor. She runs to the book box in the living room. She brings the worn paperback to Daniel, crossing her arm over her middle. She lays the book on it, like she's displaying wine in a restaurant. Her eyes down, she nods when Daniel takes the book.

He says, "I'm gonna do the O sounds, Mama, but only the good ones this time." Suzette sits with her chin on the table, closes her eyes for the full effect. Daniel begins. "O-V-E, also see O-F. Above, belove, boxing-glove, shove, turtle-dove, unglove." Suzette's eyes are still closed, feet swinging in lazy comfortable eights.

She smiles, "That's a good one, Danny." We nod. "Do rabbit, do kitten, Danny." Her feet twirl faster under the table.

"Do home," I say, spooning the weak batter into the pan.

"O-M-E, also see O-A-M. Chrome, home, metronome, Rome, St. Jerome, tome." As I listen, I think of the man I knew who gave Danny this poetry book, back when Suzette was still crawling. He presented it then just the way Suzette does now; like a fine wine. He told us that book had all the poems in the world in it; *'Capricorn Rhyming Dictionary, Daniel—It'll serve you well, boy'*. It's funny how ghosts walk by, tap your shoulder every so often. I haven't thought about that guy since Suzette started wearing glasses. A college kid, she got his eyes.

Danny can't find rabbit or bunny for her, so he's winging it, "—bumblebee, chick-a-dee, chimpanzee, fancy-free, mulberry tree." I scrape the last of the jam from the jar with a rubber spatula and spread it thin on the hotcakes.

"Suzie, baby, put the forks and cups on the table.

Danny, you do the milk."

I roll three slim pancakes for them, sprinkling the last of the confectioner's sugar over the top. I hate this dinner, hate the space on the plate that's missing green vegetables, or potatoes, hate hearing the echoes of the worker's *tsk-tsk* as I bring the plates to the table. My eyes sting, my throat burns. I set the two half-empty plates down for this last meal.

"Mama!" Suzette kicks her chair back. She grabs hold of my legs, squeezing with all she has. Her voice is smothered in the bend of my jeans; she says to my pocket, "Mama, you're the best-est Mama in the land. Pancakes for dinner. Bumblebee! Chimpanzee!" She throws her arms out to spin around. Bumps the milk from Daniel's hand. I'm too late to reach and stop the carton from bouncing, flowing onto the table in a white flood. Milk from her cup follows the arc of Suzette's hand out, over the table to the floor.

In an instant rage overtakes me. I want to grab and shake all the play out of her. Shake her till she screams. Shake all my responsibility full out of her. I grab for her shoulders. Set her down hard in Daniel's chair.

Daniel already has a dish towel to sop up the milk. Suzette's glasses are pushed off from her nose. But she leaves them like that, afraid to move. I get another rag from the sink, return to the table to see her shoulders are hunched. Unsure. Her lips move, repeating silent numbers, *3-3-7-2-7-0-1.*

In just that second the milk carton and my patience empty out. I want to run from the house, as fast as milk runs down the table leg. To escape the mishaps, and bad planning, the things that just keep happening. Away. But those shoulders signal to me.

I pick Suzette up into my arms, rock her side to side, crooning into her wild black hair, until she starts to shake with little hiccup-y sobs. "It's OK, Suz, it's OK. You didn't do anything wrong. It just happened. No one's to blame. I'm just not quick enough anymore." We pace around the kitchen; Daniel rights the chair on the floor. "See, Daniel's got it cleaned up already. See?"

I pat a chair for Daniel. "Sit," I whisper, and take the other place, Suzette in my lap. My hands shake when I hand her the fork, bring her plate closer to her chin. "Eat, baby." She finishes dinner sitting that way, on my lap. Which is good, cause this way she won't see my eyes. I can't keep them dry, but only Daniel sees. Suzette reaches for her empty cup, forgetting the milk is already gone.

Suzette dunks her plastic lion under the bath water, then uses both her thumbs to wipe all the soap from its eyes. I taught her how to do that. Quick, so the soap won't sting. That's something she got from me. I lean to kiss her slick forehead. She chants to her lion, "Bumblebee, chimpanzee." Poems, that's something she'll take with her. I guess that's a thing to hold onto. The lion dances under her hand, wet, along the edge of the tub. Suzette sings the song from the radio. I sit back on my heels. *Oh, my God.* The lion dances on.

After Suzette's bath and more bumblebee, chimpanzee, I turn out their light and sit in the dark, on the floor. I keep talking to them, waiting till I hear they're both breathing deeply. But Danny's still not asleep. What's he waiting for?

The only thing coming is the morning. I want to go now, leave them here for the worker to come find. I'm drained from the wait. I want to go quickly, not the way my life is bleeding away, days at a time, farther and farther out of my own reach.

But I don't go. I stay. I sing low for Danny, in the darkness a while longer, that tune from when he was a baby. I wait for his sleep breathing to come. I think about hospitals they don't just let you walk out of. Suzette with her phone number. Daniel with Suzette.

Daniel rises up on an elbow, reaches for me in the dark, he says, "In the hospital, Mama—keep the radio near your bed, so you can sing till you're sleepy."

"I will," I promise.

I hold his hand. Kneel and kiss his forehead. I think: what do good mothers say? 'Don't lie? Be nice?' He seems too small, trying to be so brave. What more can I say he doesn't already know?

I wonder if I can ever make myself whole again. I wonder how long it will take Suzette to forget 3-3-7-2-7-0-1 and the songs for her lion.

Dandruff as Tall as Donald Duck

FOR MOST OF that first week, I kind of felt it was doable. Me staying put.

I really thought I was going to be okay. But then, Sam did that thing with his dandruff from Monday all the way till Thursday night. That Thursday, fourteen nights into my captivity, Sam sat at the dinner table for, like, two full hours; right after sundown till we heard Mom tell Jessie to go to bed. That was what, 8:30?

And still there he was; patient, busy, eyes down on the opened newspaper under his elbows. Shoulders scrunched low, scratching and scratching till this mound of sloughed-off dandruff flakes sat waiting; a pile two fingers wide and maybe three high. Just sitting there.

Jessie's stomping, past the table, crumpled his little grey mound. An eleven-year-old earthquake goddess heading off to bed, smiting mortals and dead follicles along the way. But once she passed him, Sam, un-wearied, fluffed the pile back up with the tips of his fingernails, curling the newspaper up from each corner.

My knapsack sits by my bedroom window. None of us ever gives up. And that realization keeps working deep in my chest, from opposite sides. So talking myself into staying; that was a big thing. But then, here was Sam and this growing pile of dandruff; building it higher and higher over four days. It was the patience of it all. Doing something so diligently, for some plan that had to be so wrong.

Liz passed Jessie in the hall and Mom shouted at her. "Put that banana back. Now."

"But, I've already opened it," Liz said.

"*Opened,* my foot. Use some cling-wrap and put it back. It's for Danny's lunch."

Danny. The nearly step-dad. And my sometimes champion. Liz froze, holding the banana, "It's all there is to eat in there. I'm hungry."

"*Eat,* my foot—" Mom started in again.

And in the silence that followed all you heard was Sam at the table and his *scratch, scratch, scratch.* Liz took the high road on Mom's last, "Jeez. What'er we, on rations now?" Doing some stomping of her own.

Mom said she was sick of a house full of teenagers. Like she never dreamed that's what we'd end up being when she was popping us out, one a year, way back when. "I may drown that last one, my own self."

And Jessie, bless her (Mom's voice has range), shouted from her room off the hall, "Not if I do it first!" Mom, of course, acted like nothing stirred the air.

Sam just calmly kept up with his *scratch, scratch, scratch.*

Occasionally looking to Joey, clicking through his channels, on the couch. I sat down at the table, thinking about the months I'd been free, out of this zoo and asked Sam, "Lemme, guess. A bet?"

"Nope."

"Okay, then what?" I said it like I really was trying. Like my worker had made me promise I'd do. But he wouldn't budge.

"You'll see," Sam said to the newspaper.

And Mom says to Joey, "Turn that damn thing down or off. Those're your choices, mister." I told no one in particular that I was going to bed. And mom gave me her evil look. But I just shrugged, didn't even look back. Her voice followed me down the hall, "Oh, that's right. Isolation. Good call, Reina." But she didn't mean that. She was just on auto-pilot tonight. If she'd meant to be hateful she'd ignore me. Not even raise her shoulders to the sound of my voice.

Liz got really pissed off. Me coming into what she saw now as *her room.* "Pick up your stuff, or out it goes," she said, about my knapsack, waiting under the window.

"Very good," I said. "Very Mom-like, lots of bile. Seven-point-nine. I think you're nearly there, Liz."

"Loser."

"Ouch." I fell onto my *new* bed. "She cuts me."

So Liz thought a bit. "Go get me that banana and you can have all your drawers back."

From this bed I saw her face in the mirror on the closet door. I'd never seen her from this view and we'd lived in this room for ten years now. She seemed sad. I couldn't figure out if I knew then I couldn't stay. If her sadness was hunger or not.

A half hour later I just had to know why Sam was doing it. So I made my way back to the dining room table. I sat and fiddled with the salt and pepper shakers, Minnie Mouse and Donald Duck, on the stained table cloth. "It's for Joey, right?"

"Great minds." He grinned down at his little Matterhorn of dandruff. "Missed you, Reina."

I sat back like someone had punched me, picturing mom and Liz, and Sam and even little Jessie, rolling, holding the giggles deep inside themselves, pointing in silence at poor Joey sitting oblivious to us all, watching his TV shows, and not even noticing; with Sam's little pile of dandruff as tall as Donald Duck dumped on his head.

What was it that did it? Knowing I thought the same way all of them did? Or hating myself for figuring out that I did?

I walked into the kitchen, looked around and decided.

I pushed Danny's soda for his lunch, the cling-wrapped banana, and three tortillas into the pouch pocket of my hoodie then made my way back to the bedroom.

"Here." I tossed the food on what used to be my bed. Liz didn't even say thanks. I looked around one last time and then pulled open the window and tossed my knapsack out. This was it. I knew this was doable. Me going for real. Before I jumped I turned to Liz, for what it was worth, 'cause none of us in this family ever give up.

"Be good to each other, damn it."

ACKNOWLEDGEMENTS

"I am not I; thou art not he or she: they are not they."
—Evelyn Waugh

The Author is grateful to Catherine Ryan Hyde, Yvonne Nelson Perry, Leonard Tourney, Carol Bolton, Brent Ghelfi, James Sallis, Craig Holden, Gail Lavender and Don Waters. Writers yes, but also teachers and mentors. My work and I are in your debt.

Thanks also to Sara-Jayne Slack for allowing this small gem the opportunity to shine.

ABOUT THE AUTHOR

E.J. Runyon lives in the US Southwest. Since 2002 she's found herself moving on to smaller and smaller desert towns, while working to become the author and writing coach she planned to be.

First, she quit working in software and sold her home to finance her degree in Creative Writing and her Grad-work in Online Teaching and Learning. She's never looked back. Now, her life revolves around her own writing and online coaching business Bridge to Story, and you know, being a better person day to day.

Find the author via her website: www.ej-runyon.com

Or tweet at her: @EJRunyon

MORE FROM THIS AUTHOR

A House of Light & Stone
Nominated for the 2015 Golden Crown Literary Society Dramatic Fiction Award

Swimming against the tides of her troubled family as well as her own cultural identity, Duffy struggles with the cards she has been dealt. Buoyed up by the belief of a select few, she strives to achieve the kind of self-knowledge that comes so naturally to the 'real girls' all around her. As gaps in the narrative begin to fill, and the truth surrounding Duffy's birth is unearthed, her determination to succeed is rendered all the more astounding.

Told in uncompromising clarity through the eyes of a child, A House of Light & Stone is at once full of heartbreak and hope, offering respites of warmth in the coldest of places.

Tell Me (How To Write) A Story
You might have already begun writing something you've had a great idea for. But a great story requires more than the gift of inspiration. Tell Me (How To Write) A Story takes you through the first steps of what you need to know to write well, and how to improve your editing technique.

Other Titles:
Your Little Red Book
Good People
5 Ways of Thinking to Turn Your Writing World Around

Available from all major online and offline outlets.